KT-442-869

THE GRUNTS
in Trouble

Look out for:

Philip Ardagh
THE GRUNTS
in Trouble

Illustrated by
Axel Scheffler

nosy crow

For FCRC,
with thanks for his permission
to use the name "Ginger Biscuit"

First published in the UK in 2012 by Nosy Crow Ltd
The Crow's Nest, 10a Lant Street
London, SE1 1QR, UK

Nosy Crow and associated logos are trademarks and/or registered
trademarks of Nosy Crow Ltd

A CIP catalogue record for this book is available from the British Library

Printed and bound in the UK by Clays Ltd, St Ives Plc

Papers used by Nosy Crow are made from wood grown
in sustainable forests.

ISBN: 978 0 85763 069 8

www.nosycrow.com

Check out the buzz at
www.meetthegrunts.com

CONTENTS

Chapter One
Meet the Grunts

Mr Grunt woke up with his head down by the footboard and his feet up by the headboard. He didn't realise that he'd got into bed the wrong way round the night before, so he thought someone had turned the room round in the night. And who did he blame? His wife, Mrs Grunt, of course.

Mr Grunt was FUMING. He reached over the side of the bed and, feeling something fluffy and stiff, curled his hairy fat fingers around it. It was Ginger Biscuit's tail. Ginger

1

Biscuit wasn't a biscuit and, although he was great-big-ginger-cat-shaped, he wasn't a great big ginger cat either. Ginger Biscuit was a doorstop: a doorstop stuffed with sawdust and *very heavy* (as doorstops should be). Mrs Grunt loved that old cloth moggy so much that she made Mr Grunt stuff him with fresh sawdust every time he sprung a serious leak. (Whenever Mr Grunt refused, she hid his favourite hat in the back of the fridge until he did.)

Mr Grunt struggled out of bed and stomped over to the window, accidentally brushing Ginger Biscuit's tail against Mrs Grunt's nose. She was snoring like an old boiler about to break down any minute, and had her mouth half open showing a jumble of yellow and green teeth. "Wh— What?" she spluttered, sitting up with a jolt. "What are you playing at, mister?"

"Teaching you a lesson, wife!" grunted Mr Grunt, opening the window and throwing the stuffed cat straight out of it.

Mrs Grunt watched it go with a mixture of puzzlement and anger. "Lesson? What lesson?" she demanded. (She had hated lessons at school, except for science when she could make explosions – she *loved* a good explosion – and certainly didn't want Mr Grunt teaching her a lesson first thing in the morning.) She swung her legs over the side of the bed and rammed her feet into a moth-eaten pair of old bunny slippers.

"I can't remember what lesson!" said Mr Grunt, which was true. He couldn't. "I want my breakfast."

(I don't usually eat breakfast myself, but there are those people who say that it's the most important meal of the day. One thing you can be sure of, though, is that people who say that about breakfast have *never* eaten one of the Grunts' breakfasts.)

Mrs Grunt snorted. "Then MAKE some breakfast," she said.

"But it's your turn!" Mr Grunt insisted. "I made us that lovely badger porridge yesterday morning." (The Grunts usually made meals from things they found squashed in the road. Squashed squirrels were a favourite, but even old car tyres didn't taste too bad to them, if they added enough salt and pepper.)

"It was badger STEW, not porridge," grunted

Mrs Grunt, "and you made it for *lunch* not breakfast, so it's YOUR TURN."

"Huh!" grunted Mr Grunt grudgingly. Mrs Grunt was right. He could now remember the bird-seed-and-sawdust cereal she'd served up the previous morning. Not bad. Not bad at all. He watched her stomping off in those tatty old bunny slippers of hers. She looked beautiful. Well, she looked beautiful to *him*. "Where are you going?" he demanded.

"I've got a cat to collect," said Mrs Grunt. She stepped out of the bedroom, tripped over something on the landing and promptly fell down the stairs.

"Argh!"

Bounce.

Boing!

THUD !

(Another)

"*Argh !*"

Roll.

(An even bigger)

"*Argh !*"

The something she'd tripped over was
Sunny. Sunny wasn't the Grunts' flesh-and-
blood child. They didn't have one of their
own, but Mrs Grunt had always wanted one
and on one of those rare occasions when Mr
Grunt was in a good mood and feeling all
lovey-dovey towards his wife, he'd got her

one. Well, *stolen* one. (Not that he'd planned it, you understand. Oh no, it wasn't planned. It kind of just *happened*.)

Mr Grunt had been out pounding the pavement in search of something else – I've no idea what – when he'd glanced over a garden wall (or maybe a fence, he could never remember which) and caught sight of a washing line. On that washing line had been an assortment of things hanging up to dry, one of which he was pretty sure was a spotted sock and another of which had been a child. The child was held in position by large, old-fashioned clothes pegs clipped to each ear. And before you could say, "Put that child back, it's not yours . . . and, anyway, it's not dry yet!" Mr Grunt had leaned over the wall (or fence) and whipped that child off the line.

Mrs Grunt had been very pleased. Sunny

was the best present Mr Grunt had ever given her (with the possible exception of a pair of very expensive gold-coloured sandals and some old taped-together barbecue tongs, which she used to pull out her nose hairs). Mrs Grunt didn't know much about children but she could tell this one was a boy.

Mrs Grunt knew that boys should always be dressed in blue so she took a bottle of blue ink out of Mr Grunt's desk and tipped the contents into a great big saucepan full of boiling water. Next, she found some of her old dresses back from when she was a little girl and added them to the mix. She'd kept the dresses to use as cleaning rags, but now they were dyed they didn't look bad. Then, because she didn't like to waste things, she went on to serve up the boiling blue water to Mr Grunt, who'd liked it so much he had seconds. But he wasn't so happy when he had a blue tongue and blue lips for eight weeks.

Sunny was already an odd-looking boy, what with his left ear being higher than his right ear and that kind of sticky-up hair which NEVER goes flat, even if you pour glue into it and then try taping it into position with rolls of sticky tape, but in a badly made, badly dyed blue dress he looked really, REALLY odd.

Here, let me spell that for you:

O - D - D.

(Perhaps you could jot it down on a piece of paper and keep it under your beard until I ask you for it later. If you don't have a beard

then perhaps you could ask for one for your birthday.)

Sunny had been very young when Mr Grunt had snatched him from that washing line, so he didn't remember much about his real parents. He couldn't remember his father at all (though he did have a memory of a pair of amazingly shiny polished black shoes). As for his mother, what he seemed to remember most about her was a nice warm snuggly feeling and the smell of talcum powder. Once in a while, snatches of a song would drift into his mind on little wisps of memory. The song was something to do with fluffy little lambs shaking their lovely little lambs' tails, and – in his mind – it was his mother singing it. She had the voice of an angel who'd had singing lessons from a really good teacher.

The Grunts were very fond of Sunny in their

own way, but their own way was a *strange* way. Let me give you some examples (and if you don't like my examples you can always give them back).

For example: Mr and Mrs Grunt knew that boys don't like washing, so they never made Sunny wash. They knew that boys don't like tidying their bedrooms, so they didn't give him a bedroom. They made him sleep on the landing outside *their* room.

The truth be told, there wasn't room for a second bedroom in the Grunts' house because they didn't live in an ordinary house. They lived in a caravan.

Not a lovely, pretty, brightly painted wooden caravan.

No, not one of those. Put such thoughts out of your mind.

Nor a sleek, modern, metal caravan.

No, not one of those either.

They lived in a caravan Mr Grunt and his dad (Old Mr Grunt) had built together out of *stuff*. Stuff that included an old garden shed, the sidecar of a motorbike-and-sidecar, the less interesting half of an ice-cream van and some bobs (from a collection of bits and bobs) including an old dog kennel, some wooden planks and a frothy-coffee-making machine. The end result usually made most sensible people run away if they saw it being towed round the corner by the Grunts' two donkeys, Clip and Clop.

Ah, Clip and Clop. I was wondering when I'd get a chance to tell you about them, and now here we are.

Clip and Clop were sister and brother and/or brother and sister. They both had ridiculously long, lovable ears and big, lovable noses.

For a long time the Grunts thought that there was only one of them – that they were one and the same donkey – and they called "it" Clip-Clop. It was only when Sunny pointed out they could see them both at once, next to each other, that they realised that there must be TWO donkeys.

(This may not make much sense to you or me, but it's the Grunts we're talking about here, remember. They're not like the rest of us. Well, certainly not like ME. I can't be sure about you, come to think of it. I've no idea how ODD you may be. Which reminds me. I hope you've still got that piece of paper tucked safe and sound under your beard.)

The easiest way to tell Clip from Clop at a glance was to imagine that their ears were the hands of a clock. Clip's ears appeared to be saying eleven o'clock and Clop's said one o'clock. If you've no idea what I mean – and, amazingly, this does happen sometimes – here's a picture to explain it.

See? Good.

It was one of Sunny's many jobs to unhitch Clip and Clop from the caravan every evening so if the donkeys decided to go for a little wander in the night, the Grunts' house stayed put.

Back in the days before Mr Grunt took Sunny from the washing line and gave him to Mrs Grunt, it was up to them to unhitch the pair. And as you've probably realised by now, Mr and Mrs Grunt aren't the two most reliable people in the world.

More often than not, Mr Grunt would think that Mrs Grunt had unhitched the donkeys and Mrs Grunt would think that Mr Grunt had done it, so the job wouldn't get done and they'd wake up MILES from where they thought they'd parked their house the night before.

On one memorable occasion they woke up

on a golf course to find Clip sticking her nose down one of the holes, Clop thoughtfully chewing the little flagpole next to it, and a VERY angry, VERY red-faced man running towards them with a double-barrelled shotgun.

Mr Grunt knew that it was a double-barrelled shotgun because the man was firing at them WITH BOTH BARRELS! It took Mrs Grunt a week to dig the buckshot – the little round pellets inside the shotgun cartridges – out of Mr Grunt's bottom with a pair of rusty eyebrow tweezers. (And please don't ask me how you get rusty eyebrows because that'll make me almost as angry as the golf-club groundsman had been with them and the donkeys.) Mrs Grunt had a big grin on her face every time Mr Grunt went "Ouch!" as she dug out another tiny pellet, but that's not to say she didn't secretly love him as much as he secretly loved her. (Shocking, I know, but true.) How much Mr and Mrs Grunt loved Clip and Clop was unclear. Lately, Sunny had heard Mr Grunt grumbling about the pair "not being as hard-working as they used to be" and muttering, "What good are donkeys that won't do the donkey work?"

Now, where were we?

Oh, yes.

When Mrs Grunt tripped over Sunny outside the bedroom door and went tumbling down the stairs, she ended up tumbling out of the doors of the caravan and on to the ground. She narrowly avoided a patch of extremely

19

stingy stinging nettles but did land head-first in a mole hill.

"If you're going to fall downstairs, then do it *quietly*, wife!" Mr Grunt shouted from the bed. "Some of us have more sleeping to do." He pulled the duvet over his head, rolled over and fell on to the floor.

He landed on Sharpie, Mrs Grunt's stuffed hedgehog. A real one.

"OUCH!" yelled Mr Grunt.

His cry of pain could be heard as far away as Bigg Manor (if you were an exotic bird with very good hearing). That's BIGG MANOR, with two Gs. But more about *that* later.

Lots more.

Chapter Two.
Throwing Things

By the time Mr Grunt had got back into bed and Mrs Grunt had clambered back inside the caravan, her beloved Ginger Biscuit tucked under her arm, Sunny had given Clip and Clop their breakfast and hitched them up to the front of the van. It was time to head off again. He walked alongside the donkeys as they slowly moved forward, pulling the huge weight of the caravan behind them.

The sun was shining and birds sang in the trees. Well, *some* birds, at least. Others were

busy trying to pull reluctant juicy breakfast worms out of the ground, and yet more of them were flying away in horror at the sight of the Grunts' home-made caravan trundling along the asphalt road. Their little beaks were all a-quiver.

Mr and Mrs Grunt never really seemed to care much where they went, as long as they were going *somewhere*, though sometimes Mr Grunt would leave them for a few days – often on a rusty old bike made up from the parts of three separate rusty old bikes – then miraculously find them, wherever they'd ended up.

The Grunts didn't like staying in one spot for too long because whenever they did, they usually ended up getting into trouble. They didn't MEAN to, but they didn't go out of their way to avoid it either – like the time they walked through the middle of a re-enactment of a famous battle involving three thousand people dressed as soldiers, and there was something about the way they joined in that seemed to upset people.

And not just people.

Sometimes animals too.

Once Mr Grunt upset a glow worm so much that it deliberately kept him awake all night by hovering above his bed, flashing on and off, on and off.

(And I suspect you're beginning to get an idea of *just* how irritating that can be. I went to make myself a cup of coffee part way through.)

Soon the Grunt residence was trundling up a hill, which was quite hard work for Clip and Clop but they didn't seem too bothered. Sunny had made sure that they'd had a good feed before they went to sleep and a good feed when they woke up – and the sleep in between had been peaceful – so they were in a good mood. Sunny was wandering along beside them, but before starting the uphill climb had double-checked that the bottom part of the stable-like door to the caravan (at the back) was bolted shut.

Why?

I'll tell you why. (That's what I'm here for, as well as to add a bit of bearded glamour.) He checked that it was bolted because if it hadn't been, once the caravan started going uphill the door might have swung open and lots of stuff would have rolled out of the doorway and into the road . . . which is what used to happen a lot before Sunny became part of the family.

Unfortunately, Mr Grunt had decided to have a bath. He was sitting in the tin tub just before the whole caravan had tilted backwards and begun the climb. The tub was fixed to the floor, so there was no problem with it sliding about, and it had a detachable lid with a hole for his head to stick out of so the water didn't slop everywhere, but he had left a big cake of soap resting on the floor.

Now the soap slid across the floor and right into the path of Mrs Grunt. Mrs Grunt wasn't one for looking where she was going even at the best of times. At that particular moment, however, she was carrying some rolls of turf she'd borrowed from a village green – which was now more of a village *brown*, because without its lovely layer of grass it looked plain muddy – so she couldn't have been watching her step even if she'd wanted to. She stood on the cake of soap, which skidded away in front of her, taking one foot forward and leaving the rest of her behind, like an ice-skater doing the splits.

She landed on top of the lid of the tin bath with a resounding CLANK (or THUNG!). The noise was like the sound you might get from a very fat knight in a roomy suit of armour being hit on the breastplate with a big, spiky truncheon-like thingy.

Next, the rolls of turf that had been in her arms went flying up in the air and came flopping down on her and on Mr Grunt and

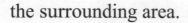

the surrounding area.

"Idiot woman!" said Mr Grunt.

"Rude man!" said Mrs Grunt. She had just spied the cake of soap on the floor and realised what must have happened. "This is your fault."

"Yours."

"Yours!"

"Yours!"

"Yours!" Mrs Grunt repeated, just as Sunny appeared through the doorway. He had heard the terrible CLANG (or THUNG!), stopped Clip and Clop as soon as he reached a not-quite-so-steep part on their uphill journey, and had come to investigate.

"Your father tried to trip me up," she protested.

"But he's in the bath," Sunny pointed out, "so how could he?"

"Through trickery!" cried Mrs Grunt. "That's what it was! Trickery!"

Sunny looked from the roll of turf on top of Mrs Grunt's head to the roll of turf on top of Mr Grunt's head and then back again. "Why are you both wearing grass wigs?" he asked. Mr Grunt gave out a big grunt and flung his piece of turf across the room. It landed on the doorstop cat, knocking him sideways.

"Ginger Biscuit!" cried Mrs Grunt, struggling off the bath lid and hurrying over to her beloved sawdust-filled moggy.

Sunny sighed and, safe in the knowledge that everything was pretty much normal (as far as the Grunt family was concerned, that is), went back outside – carefully bolting the bottom half of the stable-style door behind him – and returned to Clip and Clop.

Ten minutes or so later, Sunny found himself

leading the donkeys down the country road
that led past the entrance to Bigg Manor.
(Remember the name?

B-I-G-G ? Yes, that one.)

Up ahead a tallish, thinnish man was
standing in the middle of the road with a neat
pyramid-shaped pile of rocks. His name was
Larry Smalls and he was wearing a badly
crumpled, coal-black top hat on his head (of
all places) and an old white T-shirt. On the
T-shirt were the words:

"BIGG AIN'T BEST"

in faded red letters.

"Hello, kid," said Larry Smalls as the

caravan approached. (The truth be told, he couldn't tell whether the child with the wonky face, sticking-up hair and blue dress was a girl or a boy.) "Want to throw a rock?"

"Where?" asked Sunny.

"Here," said Larry Smalls, pointing to the pile. "One of these."

"I meant where should I throw it?" asked Sunny.

Larry Smalls sighed. "At the gates to the Bigg house, of course," he said, looking as sad as a box of ignored kittens.

Sunny looked over at the impressive entrance to the long and winding driveway leading up to the manor house: two big brown stone pillars either side, topped with white stone lions, and two gates of black metal railings with impressive gold-coloured spikes on top.

He looked back at Larry Smalls in his BIGG AIN'T BEST T-shirt. "Excuse me," he said a little hesitantly, "but WHY, exactly?"

"Why?" said Larry Smalls with a gasp. He was wondering a "Why?" of his own. He was wondering why this odd boy – he'd worked out Sunny was a boy – was wearing a strange blue dress. (Or *any* kind of dress, come to that.)

"Why would anyone want to throw rocks at the gates?" asked Sunny.

If you must know, Sunny was very tempted to throw a rock or two. He knew that throwing rocks at things was usually wrong, but there wasn't any rock-throwing in his life, and the neat pyramid-shaped pile of them did look very *throwable*.

Each rock was roughly the size and shape of a tennis ball; just the sort of size you'd want a chuckable rock to be. (Not that I EVER throw rocks, even when one seems to be saying, *"Throw me! Throw me!"* in a tiny voice inside my head which only I can hear.)

"Why should you throw them at the gates?" said Larry Smalls. "You ask me WHY?" He looked a mixture of puzzled and outraged and a bit like one of those birds that stands on one leg just because it can. "Because that is the gateway to the home of the Bigg family. *That's* why."

"Which big family?" asked Sunny, which was yet another perfectly reasonable question.

"Not *a* big family," said Larry Smalls, who had picked the topmost rock off his pyramid-shaped pile of rocks with his long, thin fingers and was now tossing it from one hand to the other. "THE Bigg family. The family called Bigg."

"Oh," said Sunny, though his "oh" made it obvious that he wasn't any clearer as to why this meant that he should throw rocks.

Except, perhaps, for the fun of it.

Looking at the man's expression, though, Sunny didn't think that FUN had anything to do with it. He eyed Larry Smalls' T-shirt. "So the 'BIGG' on your T-shirt means the Bigg family then?" He'd assumed it had just been a case of bad spelling.

"Humph," said Larry Smalls. The smell of his breath somehow reminded Sunny of the smell of a *circus*, which was rather strange. "Don't you know your history, boy?" he asked.

Not having been to school, Sunny didn't know much about anything except what Mr

Grunt, Mrs Grunt and Mr Grunt's dad (Old Mr Grunt) had told him, along with the things he'd learned for himself over the years, of course.

And one of the most important things that he'd learned for himself was to believe *half* of what Mr Grunt, Mrs Grunt and Mr Grunt's dad (Old Mr Grunt) told him.

Sunny was just about to get an answer as to why it might be a good idea to throw rocks at the gates to Bigg Manor, when Mrs Grunt went and spoiled it all.

She appeared in the doorway of the caravan. For some strange reason – if there *was* a reason – she had a mouldy old carrot stuck in her unkempt hair. "You're blocking the road, big nose!" she shouted.

Larry Smalls – whose nose was no bigger than Mrs Grunt's – looked rather startled. He was about to protest when Mr Grunt stuck his head out of a window in the roof. "Why have we stopped, wife?" he shouted. "What have you done NOW?"

"I haven't done nothing but *breathe*," said Mrs Grunt, "and everyone has to breathe."

"Except for dead people," snapped Mr Grunt, leaning dangerously far out of the window.

"Except for dead people," his wife agreed.

"*And* except for rocks and fridges and stuff," Mr Grunt added. Because he doesn't know much about anything, this felt like a very clever conversation he was suddenly having with Mrs Grunt. Quite *intellectual*, in fact.

Clip and Clop brought him back to earth with a bump.

Quite a big bump.

They had decided that it was high time to

walk forward a few donkey paces, causing Mr Grunt to lose his balance, fall out of the window and bounce off the caravan roof on to the road.

He stood up, adjusted his belt (which his father had made for him out of two smaller belts sewn together) and stood next to his wife.

"WHAT ARE YOU DOING BLOCKING OUR WAY?" Mr Grunt shouted at Larry Smalls.

Before Larry Smalls had a chance to say anything about Bigg not being best, Mr Grunt marched over to him in six purposeful strides and tripped over the pyramid of rocks almost as though he'd done it on purpose.

Mr Grunt hit the ground like a sack of mummified cats, with a terrific THUD! and an accompanying GRUNT! The rocks went everywhere: some flying through the air, some rolling across the ground and just about ALL of them heading for Larry Smalls.

Yelping like a cartoon dog who's had his tail nipped by a crab, Smalls ran for safety. He took a giant leap and scrabbled to the top of his intended target: one of the gates to Bigg Manor.

"Lunatics!" he shouted, shaking one fist as he held on to a gold-painted spike at the top of the gate with the other. "You're all lunatics!"

Somehow the wiry man's belt had got tangled up in the spikes, looping around one of them. He was stuck, and in trying to wriggle free, lost his grip and found himself hanging from the top of the gates like a dog's chew toy on a display hook in a pet shop. The "BIGG AIN'T BEST" on his T-shirt was now facing downwards.

Mrs Grunt twisted her head round to try to read the letters the wrong way up. "Bigg ain't best at *what*?" she demanded. She didn't like it when other people knew something she didn't, which was most of the time.

"Bigg ain't best because I is!" shouted Mr Grunt, and laughed as though he'd just said the funniest thing in the world.

Mrs Grunt certainly found it funny and laughed so much that her yellow teeth – and even some of her green ones – rattled inside her head.

Now Larry Smalls' already crumpled top hat fell from his upturned head to the ground, revealing a bald patch. It landed upright. Moments later, Mr Grunt was wildly throwing Smalls' carefully selected rocks at it.

"You shouldn't throw rocks!" said Mrs Grunt scornfully. "That's dangerous." She grabbed the one from Mr Grunt's hand and threw it as hard as she could at the hat, snatching another off the ground. Fortunately for Larry Smalls, despite the Grunts being such terrible shots, none of the rocks accidentally hit him.

In fact, the only person to get hit by one of the rocks was Sack, Lord Bigg's gardener. He had got up early in the morning to hide behind a really big patch of leaves and one of the rocks had gone sailing over the wall and landed on his head. He thought Lord Bigg must have thrown it, so he reluctantly headed off to find his wheelbarrow.

How Sack *hated* gardening.

Chapter Three

Bigg Manor

Bigg Manor was very big and, as you know by now, named after the Bigg family, who had lived in the manor for hundreds and hundreds of years. (Not all at the same time, of course. For one thing, it would have got ridiculously crowded. No, as the old Biggs died, younger ones took their place and then when *they* grew old and died, the next lot took over, and so on.) Now the only Bigg left in Bigg Manor was Lord Bigg. His wife, Lady Bigg (who referred to herself as "La-La"), had got fed up with him a long time ago and had moved out to live in the pigsty in the garden.

Poppet the pig already lived there, but she didn't seem to mind sharing (though she did think Lady Bigg's table manners were pretty appalling).

Don't get the wrong idea. The pigsty at Bigg Manor wasn't your average pigsty. It wasn't a small shack with a corrugated iron roof. It was a very fine pigsty built by a very famous English architect called Albert Docks, who designed the giant rabbits that were originally going to go at the bottom of Nelson's Column in Trafalgar Square in London, until it was decided to have lions instead. But it was still a pigsty.

Lord Bigg didn't miss Lady Bigg much any more, and Lady Bigg found Poppet the pig charming company compared to her husband, so all in all everyone in Bigg Manor (and the gardens) was pretty happy.

Except for the servants.

So, if you think about it, that meant that only two people (and one pig) were happy, and the rest of them were pretty miserable. And, oh yes, there were the birds in Lord Bigg's bird collection. *They* seemed happy enough but, then again, His Lordship did treat them much, much better than he did the servants.

Back in the old days, when men wore top hats – not short, crumpled ones like Smalls' – and had big beards, and the women wore layers and layers of frilly things, there were over one hundred servants working at the manor.

Now there were just five. Count them.

There was:

Peach, the red-headed butler (1)

Agnes, the cook and maid (Two jobs, one person) (2)

Jack, the handyman (also known as Handyman Jack), who used to be the boot boy (3)

Sack, the gardener (4) and

Mimi, the (newish) boot boy. Mimi was in fact a girl but there's no such title as a "boot girl", so a boot boy she was (5).

And that certainly adds up to five (unless you count at least one of them more than once, or leave one or more out.)

The Bigg family used to be very rich. They made their money from metal railings. You have to sell a lot of metal railings to make a lot of money, and that's exactly what they did.

The government had put the very first Lord Bigg in charge of coming up with a way of stopping people falling off cliffs, and he had a brainwave.

The first thing he did was get the law-makers to pass a law saying that all cliffs had to have safety railings built along the top of them.

Then he begged, stole and borrowed money to set up a factory making safety railings.

Next, he awarded this factory – *his* factory – the job of making ALL the railings to run along the tops of all the cliffs in the country.

But the first Lord Bigg's brainwave didn't end there. The final part of his brainwave was almost genius: Lord Bigg made sure that Bigg Railings were good, but not *that* good. For the first ten years after they'd been put up, they were just the sort of railings you'd want to use to stop people falling off cliffs: big and strong and railing-like. After ten years *and one week*, though, they'd go all floppy, like the stems of wilting flowers, and then droop to the ground, completely useless. This meant that every ten years the railings had to be replaced with a lot of *new* Bigg Railings! See what I mean? Clever or what?

Because different stretches of cliff top were fenced at different times – they couldn't all be done at once – there was *never* a time when the government wasn't paying Lord Bigg's safety-railings factory for more Bigg

Railings!

And so it went on for years and years and years. All the next Lord Bigg had to do – and the one after that, and the one after that, and so on – was to make sure that someone was running his factory and making railings so that the money kept on rolling in. All *he* and the Bigg family had to do was to spend, spend, spend, which was the fun part.

One day, however, the government decided to stop wasting money on fencing off cliff tops. They decided to spend the money on guns and cannons and smart new uniforms for their soldiers instead . . . and the Bigg Railings factory was left full of railings (which went floppy just over ten years after they were made) with no one to buy them.

Because the Bigg family had no idea HOW to work, having never had to give it a go,

they decided the best way to make money was by selling off some of the stuff they already had.

The latest Lord Bigg's grandfather sold off the family tropical island, the fifty-bedroom town house and a fleet of vintage motor cars. Next, Bigg's father sold off all his wife's jewellery, his silver foil collection and some of the grounds. (He'd tried to sell his wife only to find that she'd been trying to sell him at exactly the same time. And no one had wanted to buy either of them.) This left next to nothing for the current Lord Bigg to sell, except the railings factory itself and the occasional painting or piece of furniture.

Because he paid for the servants' food and drink and let them live in Bigg Manor with him, Lord Bigg really didn't like having to pay them wages as well. He thought that they should be paying *him*. But Peach, Agnes, Jack, Sack and Mimi didn't see it that way. They said they would leave if they didn't get wages, so Lord Bigg paid them *just enough* to make them stay. He also made them each sign a very complicated, official-looking contract – with plenty of rubber stamps, and a big red seal at the bottom – which stated that if they thought of leaving without permission, *they'd* owe *him* far too much money to dare try.

So they added the contract to their usual list of grumblings, stayed at Bigg Manor, and felt even more cross and miserable.

Peach the butler was usually moaning about his corns and bunions (which were lumpy things on his feet).

Agnes the cook and maid was always going on about her different allergies, which made her eyes and nose run and brought her out in all kinds of interesting spots and exciting blotches in the shapes of different counties.

Jack was forever breaking different parts of himself – arms, legs and, once, an ear – while climbing ladders when trying to mend everything from holes in the roof to a dripping tap. (This didn't put him in the best of moods.)

Sack the gardener hated plants and flowers. Actually, he hated most things. This was because he was a really good inventor. His inventions included the hat and the motor car. The only trouble was, someone had already invented hats and cars before him, and when he found this out he got terribly upset and blamed everyone and everything around him (including the daisies, marrows, peas and carrots).

And Mimi, the boot boy, found polishing everyone else's boots VERY BORING INDEED. She was also fed up with everyone calling her a *boy*, which is why she wore an ENORMOUS pink bow in her hair and pink-framed glasses with tinted pink lenses. She had also got Sack the gardener to give her all the old rose petals, which she boiled up in a big saucepan to create her very own home-made girly-smelling perfume. It smelled so sickly sweet that a quick dab behind each ear was enough to attract all the hummingbirds in the district. (All two of them. They were called Frizzle and Twist and they were part of His Lordship's bird collection.)

On top of all these gripes and groans, the servants at Bigg Manor lived in the part of the house that didn't have any glass in the windows and had very few planks on the floor. (Lord Bigg used the planks from that part of the house for firewood. I've no idea what happened to the glass.) They also had very little furniture. With the exception of the furniture in his own rooms, Lord Bigg had sold off all the valuable stuff and burned a lot of the cheaper stuff for fuel too (when he ran out of planks).

The servants' beds were made of old sacks stuffed with straw and old beard hairs.

His Lordship's rooms were nice enough, though, and he did have a best friend in Monty the parrot.

Monty the parrot was actually as grumpy as the servants but Lord Bigg didn't seem to notice. Monty bit him hard and often and it didn't seem to bother His Lordship in the slightest. He simply stuck another sticking plaster on the cut (which was why Lord Bigg

was usually covered in the things). If a servant had bitten him so much as ONCE, he'd have exploded in a terrible rage.

That day, Lord Bigg was woken up by

a squawk from Monty, who had in turn been disturbed by the distant, but still loud, "OUCH!". You know the one: it was the "OUCH!" from Mr Grunt when he'd rolled out of bed and landed on Sharpie the stuffed hedgehog. The house was at the end of  a long driveway, some distance from the road, but as well as having beady, birdie eyes Monty had *excellent* birdie hearing.

Lord Bigg slept in a huge bed that looked more like a giant wooden sledge. He sat up, let out a great big yawn, leaned against his pile of plump pillows, and yanked a bell-rope.

Down in the dark, dank kitchens, a little bell tinkled. It was the signal for Agnes to cook and take up his breakfast. She was asleep at the kitchen table (an old packing crate), her head slumped over a copy of *Dull* magazine. *Dull* magazine was a weekly magazine full of such boring articles that it was supposed to make you feel better about your own life. Agnes had been reading a piece about a woman who spent thirty-five years inside a hollow tree counting ants. Suddenly, working for the horrible Lord Bigg inside nasty Bigg Manor hadn't seemed quite so bad.

The annoying tinkling of the bell woke her up. She had been having a lovely dream about having a pet frog that burped up gold coins. When she realised that it had been just that – a lovely dream – she felt very upset, and came out in a whole new set of blotches. She dragged herself out of her chair and banged a frying pan down on to the top of the great big iron range stove to cook His Lordship his morning eggies.

Lord Bigg had finished his eggies and was sharing a piece of toast with Monty the parrot when there was yet *more* noise. This time it was the distant sound of the "thunk-phwut-thwacks" made by the Grunts' rock-throwing, and it got the parrot into another flap. He squawked and ruffled his feathers, then flew over to the window, where he tapped the glass with his beak.

"What is it, Monty?" asked Lord Bigg. He lifted the tray off his lap, threw back his bedclothes and stepped out on to a threadbare rug. "What's all the fuss about?" He slipped a blue silk dressing gown over his red-and-white striped pyjamas, and strode across to the window. Monty flapped up on to his shoulder.

With money in such short supply, Lord Bigg had bought the dressing gown second-hand from an Internet auction site. (A rather dodgy Internet site, where not everything on it was being sold by people who actually had the right to sell them, if you see what I mean. As in: they probably-weren't-theirs-to-sell.) What *hadn't* been stated in the ad was that the dressing gown must have been worn by a boxer into the boxing ring. So when it arrived and Lord Biggs unwrapped it, he was surprised to find that it had writing on the back. The big black letters said:

"Barney "The Bruiser" Brown

No wonder the photo on the website had only shown the dressing gown from the *front*.

At first, Lord Bigg had been very angry. Then he decided that, because he only ever saw himself from the *front*, it didn't really matter. What's more, Barney "The Bruiser" Brown had been quite a GOOD boxer in his day, before he had retired and got himself a new job with a smart blue uniform.

Standing at the window, Lord Bigg pulled a small pair of mother-of-pearl-coated binoculars from a dressing-gown pocket and held them up to his eyes. He surveyed the scene. Through the trees he could just make out the entrance to the grounds. What he spied was the Grunts and Larry Smalls. What he thought was: *trouble*.

Chapter Four

Bees a-Buzzin'

By the time Lord Bigg had tramped all the way out of the house and down the drive to the entrance gates, Mr and Mrs Grunt, Sunny and the donkeys were long gone.

All His Lordship found was Larry Smalls hanging from the top of one of the gates, and tennis ball-sized rocks dotted all over the ground.

"What in blazes are you doing up there, man?" demanded Lord Bigg.

"Squawk!" added Monty the parrot for good

measure.

"Bigg ain't best!" shouted Larry Smalls, who was very proud of his slogan and couldn't think what else to say anyway.

"Oh, it's *you*, is it?" said Lord Bigg with a sigh.

"Of course I'm me," said Larry Smalls.

"You're the man who threw the cauliflowers at me at the village fête, aren't you?" said Lord Bigg.

Larry Smalls nodded proudly. "And who tried to drown you at the swimming gala!" he added.

"And posted me that very realistic rubber tarantula!" spluttered Lord Bigg.

"And smeared full-fat yoghurt on the saddle of your bike!" said Larry Smalls.

"And tried to push me into that vat of marmalade on the factory outing!" said His

Lordship.

"And forced your motor car into a ditch that wet Wednesday!" Smalls nodded with glee.

"And locked me in that cupboard at the art gallery that dry Thursday!" fumed Lord Bigg.

"And—" began Larry Smalls, only to be interrupted this time.

"And I think I'll go and call the police," said Lord Bigg. He looked down at his feet. There on the ground in front of him was a coal-black, short, crumpled top hat. "Yours, I take it?" he said, looking up at Smalls.

"Mine!" agreed Smalls.

Lord Bigg picked the hat up, crumpled it some more, and somehow managed to squodge it into a large outside pocket of his dressing gown.

"You can't do that!" Larry Smalls protested.

Lord Bigg chose to ignore him.

Monty the parrot, on the other hand, took immediate action. Up until now he'd been perching on Lord Bigg's left shoulder. He flapped up into the air and sank his beak into Larry Smalls' nose.

"ARGGGGGHHHHHHH !"

screeched Mr Smalls, then added a few very rude words, which I'm FAR too polite to repeat here and now. (Maybe later, when no one else is around, if you ask me nicely.)

"I want you off my land – I mean, off my *gate* – within the hour," said Lord Bigg, "or I really will call the police. One hour."

"But I'm stuck!" protested Larry Smalls. He clutched his bleeding, swollen nose in both hands.

"That's not my problem," said His Lordship. He turned and walked away. Monty the parrot swooped low and landed back on his shoulder. From the top of the gate, his belt looped over a railing spike, Mr Smalls read the back of Lord Bigg's dressing gown with a puzzled frown.

Barney "The Bruiser" Brown?

Lord Bigg was Barney "The Bruiser" Brown?

Blimey.

Smalls hadn't even known that Lord Bigg was a boxer, let alone a fairly well-known one, recently retired from the ring. That would help explain why Bigg was covered in little crosses of sticky plasters. Boxing injuries!

Larry Smalls would never admit it, but he was impressed that Lord Bigg was Barney "The Bruiser" Brown. Only a *tiny* bit impressed, but impressed none the less.

A mile or so away, meanwhile, Mr Grunt was climbing up on to the roof of the moving caravan for a better view of the road ahead. He often sat up there and often fell off, which was usually Mrs Grunt's fault, Sunny's fault or Clip and Clop's fault, but never HIS fault. (According to Mr Grunt, that is. Funny that.)

Today was no exception; as the caravan went over a small bump, Mr Grunt found himself sliding off the roof with a "Woooooaaaaah!", which was swiftly followed by an "Ahhh! Ahh! Argh! Ouch!" as he landed in a roadside gorse bush.

A gorse bush is a very prickly bush. It has a few pretty yellow flowers, but apart from that it's just about all thorns. If he'd been a sack full of jelly, Mr Grunt would have sprung some serious leaks.

Sunny sighed and told Clip and Clop to stop. They were happy to, which surprised Sunny a little until he saw what they'd seen: an especially fine patch of roadside thistles. So while he did his best to help free Mr Grunt without getting too prickled himself, the two donkeys enjoyed a mid-morning snack.

Once freed, Mr Grunt felt a need to kick something solid. Sunny remembered the time Mr Grunt had kicked a statue in the middle of a town square. It wasn't in the middle of a town square any more. It was now in pieces in the town's rubbish dump. Not that Mr Grunt's foot hadn't suffered too. For the following three days, Mrs Grunt'd had to give him a piggyback up and down stairs, and the rest of the time he'd shuffled around on his bottom like a toddler who couldn't quite toddle (so wasn't *really* a toddler yet, I suppose).

Today, however, Mr Grunt decided to kick an electricity pylon because, apart from a couple of spindly-looking trees, it was the nearest solid thing. Electricity pylons – metal towers supporting electric cables high above ground – can be dangerous things, as Mr Grunt was about to find out. He gave the pylon a mighty kick, and guess what happened . . .

Oh, go on. Guess.

Just for me.

Mr Grunt gave the pylon such a big kick that it vibrated, making the ground vibrate, causing a swarm of bees to leave their hive in a nearby tree to find out what was going on.

Did you guess right? Of course you didn't. (And if you *did* think "bees" you're either one of those people who can see into the future, or you've read this before. And that's not proper guessing, so it doesn't count.)

So the bees swarmed out of their hive to find out what was going on and, because Mr Grunt was what was going on, they decided to take a closer look. They landed on his face, creating what looked like A GIANT BEARD OF LIVING BEES.

What Mr Grunt wanted to do was to SCREAM, but even Mr Grunt wasn't stupid enough to do that because screaming would have meant having to open his mouth. And one of the last things he wanted was a mouthful of stingy bees. It was annoying enough that a few of the bees were thinking

about exploring his nostrils. So he *imagined* himself screaming and simply went beetroot red instead.

In fact, his face went *so* red that it was enough to make Clip and Clop stop chewing their thistles and stare at him with a gleam of casual interest in their donkey eyes. Or perhaps it was the enormous buzzy beard he'd suddenly grown that attracted their attention.

Mrs Grunt, meanwhile, burst out laughing. You may have heard the phrase "to laugh like a

drain", which has always confused me because drains don't laugh. I can't really describe *what* Mrs Grunt's laugh sounded like but I can say that with her mouth that wide open it *smelled* like a drain.

"Shave that thing off, mister!" she said between the guffaws. "It makes you look stupid!"

Saying that Mr Grunt looked stupid is like saying that France is "a bit French". For Mrs Grunt to have said that Mr Grunt looked stupid, then, must have meant that he looked really, *REALLY* stupid.

Sunny, meanwhile, was taking matters more seriously. He imagined that if a lot of the bees decided to sting Mr Grunt, this would be very bad – as well as very painful – for him. So how could he help?

Sunny ran back inside the caravan and

grabbed a big jar of honey off the breakfast table. The Grunts had discovered long ago that a smear of honey could make even the toughest squashed magpie even tastier, so they'd bought the biggest jar they could find. And bees like honey, don't they? (Or is that bears?)

"Here, bee, bee, *bees*!" said Sunny, waving the open honey pot in front of Mr Grunt's buzzing face, trying to attract the stripy insects' attention. "Here, bees! Lovely honey, honey, *honey*!"

And this was the scene that met a certain young lady as she rounded the bend in the road: the strangest, most worrying-looking caravan she'd ever clapped eyes on; a cackling yellow-and-green-toothed woman; a bright-red man with an enormous beard of BUZZING BEES; and an extraordinary-looking boy, wearing an extraordinary blue dress, leaping about with a big pot of honey.

In the girl's hair was the biggest pink bow Sunny had ever seen. Yes, you guessed it: she was Lord Bigg's boot boy, Mimi. She was skipping down the lane with two tiny hummingbirds buzzing around her head like the excited bees. On seeing this most amazing sight, she stopped in her tracks and her eyes widened behind the pink-tinted lenses of her pink-framed glasses.

Waves of her cloying home-made rose-petal perfume wafted through the air. Mrs Grunt *hated* the smell. Mr Grunt couldn't smell anything except BEE. And Sunny thought it was rather nice.

But the bees?

The bees?

They LOVED IT!

Before anyone quite knew what was happening, they'd wiped themselves off Mr Grunt's face – as if he'd had an instant, magical shave – and were heading for Mimi faster than Sunny could shout, "Run for your life!"

Chapter Five
Attack!

Sack the gardener was hiding in the potting shed and he didn't want to come out. After being hit by a tennis ball-sized rock that some IDIOT had thrown over the wall, he'd gone to the shed to get ready for work, but ended up trying to get back to sleep. Lying among the terracotta pots, staring up at the cobwebby roof, he found himself inventing stuff. He just couldn't stop it.

In the space of half an hour, he'd invented the collapsible ironing board, toast, fingerless gloves and lightbulbs. Eventually, he decided that he'd better do some gardening. Unfortunately for Sack, although he really hated it, he was very good at gardening. If he threw away an apple core it would eventually grow into a tree. If he spat out a grape pip, in next to no time a vine would start curling out of the ground where it landed. He had what his gran called "green fingers".

Sack's gran (Granny Sack) was not very good at telling greens from browns, or recognising people's faces unless they were pushed up very close to her own, but she was right about the green fingers part. It's a phrase that describes someone who seems to have a natural ability to get plants to grow beautifully, without necessarily even trying that hard. (I meant the green-fingered folk don't have to try hard. The plants have to, of course. They always do. All that turning-sunlight-into-food and stuff.)

So when Sack had to garden – when there was no way out of it – he did it very well. He had just picked up his least favourite garden tools and put them in his least favourite wheelbarrow and was wheeling it across the loathsome front lawn to one of his least favourite flowerbeds when he heard Mimi.

She was sprinting down the road the other side of the wall, wailing as she went. Or was it a word? What was she saying? Was it "*Beeeeeeeeeeeeeeeeeeesss!*"?

The walls around the Bigg Manor estate were high: brick-built with no obvious foot-holds or hand-holds. Those gates with their fancy gold-topped spikes were there for a reason and not just for show. When they were closed, entrance was pretty much by invitation – or by ladder – only.

Or would have been, if there hadn't been a hole in the wall, hidden on both sides by evergreen bushes. The hole was so well hidden that Lord Bigg himself didn't know about it. But the servants, Peach, Agnes, Handyman Jack, Sack and Mimi, knew about it. And it was through this hole in the wall that Mimi suddenly appeared – well, *charged* – still crying, "*Beeeeeeeeeeeeeeeeeeeesss!*"

Sack watched in amazement as the bright-pink, rose-petal-smelling, big-bowed Mimi was pursued across the lawn by a swarm of eager bees. Hummingbirds Frizzle and Twist hovered around her ears, snapping at the buzzing insects with their tiny beaks. Moments later, a boy in a blue dress appeared through the hole, clutching the biggest jar of honey Sack had ever seen, and waving a spoon in the air.

Sunny had a dozen or so bees buzzing around him, but they obviously found Mimi *far* more interesting. Then he spotted the fish pond. There was a big lake in the grounds of Bigg Manor, but that was round the back of the house. Here at the front there was a large, formal, circular stone fish pond. It had a fountain shaped like a dolphin in the middle, which had long since stopped squirting water.

"The pond!" Sunny shouted.

"Jump into the pond!"

He wasn't sure whether Mimi had heard him. She certainly didn't veer off in that direction. So he shouted it a few more times: "Jump into the pond! Jump into the pond!"

Finally, Mimi seemed to get the message. Flapping her arms as she ran, she zigzagged across the grass, then with one last cry of "*Beeeeeeeeeeeeeeeeeeeesss!*" she threw herself into the water with an almighty SPLASH! A startled goldfish or two found themselves momentarily in mid-air, and some lily pads flew around like plates in a Greek restaurant, then all was still.

At first, Mimi kept her head above water, but the bees still swarmed around her. It was only when she ducked it below the surface that the bees lost interest and looked around for somewhere else to go. It was then that Sunny lobbed the huge jar of honey high in the air in a graceful arc. It landed on the gravel drive a fair distance away, breaking the glass and revealing a wonderful, golden, gloopy mass of honey. *Now* he had the bees' attention. They forgot all about Mimi and buzzed over to the honey.

Sunny and Sack reached the pond at about the same time. Frizzle and Twist hovered above the water where Mimi's head had disappeared moments before, their wings flapping at such a speed they seemed a blur.

As Sunny and Lord Bigg's gardener leaned over the stone surround, Mimi broke through

82

the surface of the water, gasping for air. Sack took one hand and Sunny the other and together they heaved her out on to the grass. She couldn't have looked more soaked. Her clothes clung to her like a flabby second skin, her hair dripped straight and long, and her once-proud bow looked more like a squashed, pink, soggy *something*. And gone was the smell of her rose-petal scent, to be replaced by the faintest whiff of pond water.

The first thing Mimi did was look around nervously for the bees through the pink-tinted lenses of her pink-framed spectacles.

"Don't worry about them," said Sunny, pointing towards the broken honey jar on the driveway. "That should keep them busy for a while."

Mimi's whole body suddenly seemed to sag and she lowered herself on to the stone rim of

the pond, sitting down with a bump.

"Thanks," she said, looking up at Sunny, who was panting from the chase. "Thanks for rescuing me."

"Rescuing?"

"For suggesting I jump in the pond. I would never have thought of it," said Mimi. She seemed to be taking in the boy's appearance for the first time: the sticky-up hair, the sticky-out ears and the blue dress. "I'm Mimi."

"I'm Sunny," said Sunny. "Pleased to meet you."

"And I'm Sack," said the gardener. "We'd better get away from here before His Lordship starts wondering what's going on.'

Sack headed off in the direction of his potting shed, with Sunny and Mimi following close behind. Every step she made was accompanied by a squelch from the water in her shoes.

"Do you know the man with the beard?" Mimi asked Sunny.

"What man?" asked Sunny.

"The man with the beard of bees that decided to chase me?"

"Oh," said Sunny, looking a little crestfallen. "He's my dad. He doesn't usually go around with a beard of bees. I'm pretty sure this was his first time. He kicked an electricity pylon that annoyed them, and they took a liking to his face—"

"Until I came along," said Mimi as she squelched.

"Well, you do have a much nicer face," said Sunny, then turned an interesting shade of pink when he realised what he'd just said.

"You think so?" she asked.

"Yes." He blushed some more. "And

obviously the bees thought so too. And you smell – well, you smell*ed* – fantastic."

"You liked that? It's my very own home-made rose-petal scent."

"It smelled delicious," said Sunny.

"You're not supposed to drink it!" Mimi laughed.

"You know what I mean," said Sunny.

"Yes." Mimi nodded. "I know what you mean."

"Do you work here?" Sunny asked.

"She's the boot boy," said Sack, who'd come to a halt and was fumbling for a key in his pocket.

"But she's a girl!" said Sunny.

Mimi beamed. "My point exactly!" she said, and proceeded to give Sunny a big hug, the end result being that the front half of his dress looked a far darker blue than the back half because of the wetness (and now he too had the slightest whiff of pond water about him).

Sack and Sunny waited outside the potting shed, while Mimi slipped inside, reappearing at the door a few minutes later dressed in one of Sack's overalls. "I'll put the kettle on," she said.

Soon all three were sitting around a little camping stove, three chipped enamel mugs in front of them and the kettle well on its way to boiling.

"So you live with your family in that – er – that—"

"Caravan?" said Sunny. "Yes. Dad built it himself, with a little help from *his* dad, Old Mr Grunt."

"It's unlike any caravan I've ever seen," said Mimi, which was no word of a lie.

Sunny didn't really get much of an opportunity to talk to other people so, despite the unusual circumstances, he really enjoyed his time with Mimi and Sack that afternoon. He enjoyed the tea too, when it had brewed. The so-called tea they drank back in the caravan was usually made of any old leaves Mr or Mrs Grunt decided to pick, dry and put

in the tea caddy, and Mrs Grunt sometimes simply held a corner of her dress over a cup, and poured hot water through it to give the water a bit of colour and taste. The tea he drank in the potting shed that day was real tea made from real tea leaves. It was delicious.

Sack's conversation was less enjoyable. He spent most of the time moaning about how mean Lord Bigg was, which was fair enough, I suppose, because Lord Bigg WAS very mean. He told Sunny about the servants' terrible living conditions and bad pay. And what a big old empty shell the manor really was.

"It looks so impressive from the outside," said Sunny.

"It must have been an amazing house once," Mimi agreed. "But almost everything's been sold and most of what's left has been chopped up or ripped to pieces."

"Peach and Agnes say that Lord Bigg's bedroom and sitting room are still beautiful," said Sack, "but I've never been allowed in either, what with being the gardener. My place is out here."

"And my place is down with the boots and the polish," said Mimi. Her hair was already drying out and getting some of its bounce back.

"Why don't you both leave?" said Sunny, taking his last sip of tea. "Resign? Give up your jobs?"

"We have contracts," said Sack.

"Signed documents that could land us in a load of trouble if we quit without His Lordship's permission," Mimi explained.

"You could always run away," said Sunny.

"But what would I do?" asked Sack.

"Well, you wouldn't have to garden, that's

for sure," said Sunny (who'd had an earful of just how much Sack hated, hated, *hated* gardening).

"But that's all I'm good at." Sack sighed. "If I mow a lawn I can't help doing it perfectly, even if I don't try!"

"But what would you *like* to do?" asked Sunny.

"Wait here," said Sack. He got up from the large upturned flowerpot he was using as a seat, and disappeared behind some wooden shelving, reappearing with a black plastic seed tray piled high with papers. Sitting down again, Sack grabbed a bunch of papers from the top of the pile and handed them to Sunny. "Take a look at these."

Sunny studied the beautifully drawn diagrams. There was one of a screwdriver and screw; one of a light switch; and one of a folding umbrella. All of them had their working parts carefully labelled, with lots of arrows and written explanations. "These are really well done, Sack," he said when he'd finished. "So you want to be an artist?"

"An inventor!" said Sack. "I want to invent things!"

Sunny frowned. "You – er – invented all these yourself?"

"Yes," said Sack, suddenly looking glum. "And don't tell me that someone already invented them before me, because I know that *now*. That's the trouble with all of my inventions so far!"

"But just because someone beat you to it,

doesn't mean that you're not a genius for coming up with the ideas all on your own," said Mimi.

Sack smiled again. "Mimi always says encouraging stuff like that," he said.

"She has a point," said Sunny. "What about you, Mimi?" He placed his empty mug between his feet on the potting-shed floor and twisted to face her more directly.

"What about me?" she asked.

"I mean, what would you like to do if you left Bigg Manor?"

Mimi thought for a moment, taking off her pink-framed glasses and giving the lenses a good wipe with a cloth she'd pulled from a big front pocket of her borrowed overalls. "Well," she said at last. "I love animals and I'd like to see the world, so something involving animals and travel, I suppose."

"Ah, I was meaning to ask you about those," said Sunny, pointing up at Frizzle and Twist. Now that Mimi had washed off her rose-petal perfume in the fish pond, the two hummingbirds had stopped flying around her head, but they still liked to stay close to her. They were currently hovering high above the three of them, in the pitch of the roof.

"Lord Bigg has an aviary – a bird collection," said Sack.

At that precise moment, the door to the shed was thrown open from the outside. Framed in the doorway, in brilliant sunlight, was the silhouette of a man with bushy side-whiskers

Before Sunny knew what was happening, something flapped right up to his face and pressed its big beak against his nose. It was Monty the parrot.

Sunny's eyes had quickly become accustomed to the sunlight, and he could see that the face of the man in the doorway was covered with tiny little crosses of sticking plaster.

"Who the blazes are you?" demanded Lord Bigg. He sounded far from friendly.

Chapter Six

The Fall

Lord Bigg wasn't a big fan of children. He and Lady "La-La" Bigg had once had a boy, but they'd mislaid him, which had rather pleased His Lordship and rather upset Her Ladyship. (It was one of the reasons why they were both happy with the arrangement of his living in the house and her living in the pigsty.)

There were many reasons why Lord Bigg didn't particularly like children. Firstly, they cost money. You had to feed and clothe and maybe even educate them. Then there was the fact that they didn't behave like adults. They charged round pretending to be kings or queens or aeroplanes, and had imaginary friends. They asked stupid questions, such as, "How many beans make five?" or difficult questions, such as, "Why's the sky blue?" Or stupid, difficult questions, such as, "Why aren't carrots called oranges when they're as orange as oranges are, and got here first?"

At meal times, they spent as much time *under* the table as at it, or they curled up in a ball and squirmed on their chair. More food ended up on the table, the floor and themselves

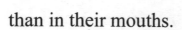

than in their mouths.

They somehow managed to get their clothes dirty within thirty seconds of putting them on. They collected bugs and mud and little scraps of paper with "important" squiggles on them.

They talked when you wanted them to be quiet and were quiet when you wanted them to say something. They gave off strange smells and said embarrassing things, such as "Why isn't Mr Morris dead yet?" when Mr Morris was standing right next to them; or "How come you have big sweat patches under your arms, Mrs Sawyer?"; or "Are you really as dumb as my daddy says you are?". And that was just for starters . . .

So no, Lord Bigg wasn't one of those lordships who wanted a son and heir who would one day take over Bigg Manor from him and keep the family name alive.

It wasn't as if he had a fortune to pass on, like in the old days when the Bigg family was still making railings. If Lord and Lady Bigg hadn't mislaid their son somewhere – and neither of them could remember which one of them had been supposed to have been looking after him when they did – he'd have inherited an empty house, some beautifully gardened gardens, a handful of servants and, probably by then, some serious debts. So it had all worked out rather well really.

Lord Bigg eyed the strange child sitting before him now. "I said, who the blazes are you?"

Sack and Mimi had jumped to their feet, and Sunny now did the same. "My name is Sunny," he said.

"And what are you doing on my land?" demanded His Lordship.

"I – er—"

"You're not with Smalls, are you?" Monty had landed on Bigg's shoulder and they both leaned forward as one, their two pairs of beady eyes boring into Sunny's. "You do look somehow familiar."

"S-S-S-malls, sir?" asked Sunny.

"An odious little man with a BIGG IS BAD T-shirt," said Bigg.

"AIN'T BEST," Sunny corrected him. "BIGG AIN'T BEST."

Lord Bigg's eyes widened and flickered with rage. "So you *are* part of his little circus."

"No!" said Sunny. "I've read the T-shirt, that's all."

Bigg looked far from convinced, and Monty was itching to bite the boy's nose. "Then who are you?"

"He saved me from the bees, Your Lordship,"

said Mimi.

"It's true, Your Lordship," said Sack. "Young Sunny here was only trying to help your boot boy, at great personal risk to himself."

"Personal risk?" Lord Bigg snorted. "I was stung by a wasp once and didn't even cry."

"But there was a whole swarm of them," Mimi protested.

"A whole hive's worth," the gardener added.

"There *were* a lot of bees, My Lord," said Sunny. He was feeling more confident now, and was distracted by all the little crosses of sticking plaster. He imagined joining them up with lines to make a picture on the man's skin, like in a dot-to-dot puzzle.

"What did you do?" said Lord Brigg. They'd caught his interest now. "Shoot them? Trap them?"

"At first I tried distracting them with honey,

but they found Mimi far more interesting," Sunny explained.

"Mimi?" asked Lord Bigg. "Who's Mimi?"

"I am, Your Lordship," said Mimi.

"Oh. And you're the boot boy, right?"

"Well, yes and no," said Mimi.

"You either are or you aren't!" said His Lordship.

"I mean I'm a boot *girl*."

Lord Bigg snorted like Poppet the pig (or Lady "La-La" Bigg). "No such thing," he said. "You're simply a boot boy who happens to be a girl."

Mimi looked sad. "Yes, Your Lordship.'

"So if the honey didn't work, what did you do?" Bigg asked Sunny.

"I made her jump in the pond. Cover herself totally with water. That did the trick."

"Clever." Lord Bigg nodded. "Where are

the bees now?"

Sunny thought of the broken jar of honey on the driveway. "We're not sure, My Lord," he said.

"They just flew off," said Sack hurriedly. "Could be anywhere."

"If I get stung, I shall hold you personally responsible," said Bigg. "Where do you live?"

"All over the place," said Sunny. "I mean, we're always on the move."

"Aha!" said Lord Bigg. "You're one of those No Fixed Abode chaps."

Of course, Sunny had NO idea what His Lordship was on about, because although he knew a "chap" was a male person, he wasn't sure what an "abode" was, fixed, broken or otherwise.

"Am I?" asked Sunny.

"You just said you were," said Bigg, nodding

his head. On his shoulder, Monty the parrot tried a little head-bobbing of his own.

"Then I must be, I suppose," said Sunny. ("No fixed abode" means "homeless", more or less.)

"So if I DO hold you personally responsible for my getting stung, and I do get stung, then it'd be a real bore having to track you down . . . so do you know what?"

Sunny didn't know what, so he shook his head. "No, My Lord," he said, "I most definitely don't know what."

"I don't think I'll hold you responsible after all. Now, please leave my property. Sack will show you out."

Sack visibly relaxed. He had been worrying that Lord Bigg might wonder how Sunny had got on to the estate in the first place, and that they might have to admit to the existence of

the hole in the wall. But it didn't seem to have occurred to him.

"Thank you," said Sunny.

Lord Bigg turned and walked away from the potting shed. Monty, however, twisted his birdie neck so that he could keep a beady eye on the newcomer as they made their exit. You could just tell he WANTED TO SINK HIS BEAK INTO THAT BOY'S NOSE.

"Well," said Sunny, once Bigg had gone a fair distance back towards the house, "I'd better be off then."

"Nice meeting you," said Sack, shaking the boy warmly by the hand. He sounded like he meant it.

"Goodbye," said Mimi. She flung her arms

round Sunny and gave him a nice dry hug this time. "It'd be very nice to see you again."

"It would," said Sunny, because it most certainly would.

Both Mimi and Sack walked with Sunny towards the main gates. They passed the broken honey jar on the driveway, but the honey appeared to have gone and there was no sign of the bees.

As they neared the gate, they could hear mutterings and the occasional yelp.

"That'll be Mr Smalls," said Sunny. "The man in the BIGG AIN'T BEST T-shirt. I'd no idea he'd still be up there."

"Should we help him get down, do you think?" asked Mimi, looking up at the man on the spikes.

"Good idea," Sunny agreed.

"Not sure how we could," said Sacks. "And anyway, if Lord Bigg wanted him down he'd have told us to do it."

"Best leave him then," said Mimi, but she didn't look sure.

Sack dug his hand in his pocket and pulled out the gate key. He turned it in the well-oiled lock and it opened with one satisfyingly smooth action, without so much as a "click". He then swung one of the gates inwards. The one with Larry Smalls on top.

"Hey! What? Who? Get me down!" Larry Smalls yelled, shaking a fist. He recognised Sunny at once (which isn't surprising with the blue dress and all). "Oh, it's YOU!"

"Ignore him," said Sack.

"IGNORE ME?" shouted Mr Smalls. "You can't ignore me!" and to make sure they didn't, he starting to sing a song about a sad clown who falls in love with a stilt-walker who's afraid of heights. Despite the fact that he was hanging from the top of a gate by his belt and that, in my opinion, the song itself was sentimental twaddle, he sounded rather good.

"Bye then!" said Sunny above the noise.

"Bye," said Mimi.

Sunny strode out on to the lane, and Sack swung the gate closed behind him (to cries of "Traitors!"). He locked the lock and slipped the key back into his pocket.

Sunny raised his arm in a final farewell, then headed off back in the direction where he'd last left Mr and Mrs Grunt.

"Don't leave me," pleaded Larry Smalls, his voice more of a whimper.

To tell the truth, Sunny felt sorry for Larry Smalls. It had been the Grunts' rock-throwing that got him stuck up there in the first place. He stopped and walked back over to the gate.

"How am I going to help you get down, Mr Smalls?" he asked. "I don't—"

"How do you know my name?" asked Larry Smalls.

"Lord Bigg called you that."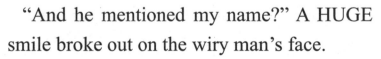

"Lord Bigg spoke to you?"

"Yes."

"And he mentioned my name?" A HUGE smile broke out on the wiry man's face.

"That's good?" asked Sunny.

"That's excellent," said Mr Smalls. "I've been bugging Bigg for years. Really trying to get under his skin. Hanging around like a

111

bad smell and he's never admitted to knowing who I am, until now . . ." He gave an even BIGGER grin.

"Er, about getting you down," Sunny reminded him. "How am I supposed to help you get down?"

"If only the Chinn Twins were here. They'd have me down in an instant. Them or Fingers."

"The Chinn Twins?"

"Oh, never mind. Those two grown-ups you were with," said Larry Smalls. "The frightening woman and the worrying man?"

"Mum and Dad, you mean?"

"They're your *parents*?" said Mr Smalls with obvious surprise.

"Near enough," said Sunny, not wanting to go into the whole taken-from-a-washing-line explanation right there and then.

"Them. Do you think you could persuade

them to come back and help me down? If they drove their – er – " He fumbled for the right word.

"Caravan?" said Sunny.

"Is that what it is?" said Larry Smalls. "If they could drive it right up against the gates, I could easily climb down from here."

Even from up there, Mr Smalls could see the doubt on Sunny's face. He thought back to Mrs Grunt's cries of "Big nose!" and their throwing rocks at his hat. "It's not going to happen, is it?" he said.

"I don't think I'd be able to persuade them, I'm afr—" Sunny began.

He was interrupted by a terrible tearing sound as Larry Smalls' belt – which had been supporting him all this time – finally gave up under the stress, and Larry Smalls came tumbling down.

In that split second, Sunny instinctively put out his arms to try to catch the man. And amazingly, Mr Smalls did land in Sunny's outstretched arms. Not surprisingly, both man and boy ended up on the ground with Sunny the worse off, because he was the one underneath. Larry Smalls rolled off him and jumped to his feet. "You caught me!" he said in amazement. "You caught me."

Sunny lay on the hard road surface gulping in new supplies of air (which was surprisingly painful).

"I can't believe you were willing to catch me!" said Mr Smalls. "Thank you. Thank you so much!"

When Sunny just carried on lying there, Larry Smalls' euphoria turned to concern. "Are you OK?" he asked.

"I'll . . . I'll . . . be . . . f-f-fine," Sunny managed.

Mr Smalls helped Sunny to his feet.

"Are you sure you're OK?"

"I'm good," said Sunny. And it was true. He felt really good. Not just good as in OK, but good as in he felt good about himself. He'd helped save Mimi from the bees and, even though it had been more of a reflex action followed by an accident, he'd helped Mr Smalls too.

Life – like honey – was sweet.

Buzz. Buzz.

Chapter Seven
Blunderbuss!

When Sunny finally caught up with Mr and Mrs Grunt they were outside the caravan about a mile and a half further down the road from where they'd been attacked by bees, having a tug-of-war with Ginger Biscuit. Clip and Clop were busy chewing some brightly coloured flowers in the flowerbed of a pretty cottage garden.

"Give it here, wife!" Mr Grunt was shouting, trying to pull the doorstop cat from Mrs Grunt's grasp.

"He's MINE," Mrs Grunt protested, "and he ain't an *it*, he's a *he*—"

"It's nothing but a moth-eaten sawdust-filled doorstop!" roared Mr Grunt (who was secretly quite fond of Ginger Biscuit too, but was never going to tell Mrs Grunt that).

"I'm back!" said Sunny.

Mr Grunt stopped tugging, causing Mrs Grunt to topple backwards on to the ground.

"HA!" laughed Mr Grunt. "Serves you right!"

"I meant to fall over," said Mrs Grunt, sitting up and dusting herself down. "I *loves* falling over . . . Where did you run off to?" she asked Sunny as she got to her feet, clutching Ginger Biscuit in one hand and rubbing her head with the other.

"I was trying to help Mimi – the girl being chased by the bees," said Sunny. Hadn't it

118

been obvious?

"You took our honey," grunted Mr Grunt.

"She needed help!" Sunny protested.

"Why?" asked Mrs Grunt. "What does she have to do with us?"

"It was Dad who kicked the pylon and that's what upset the bees," said Sunny. "We were responsible. And anyway, shouldn't we help people?"

Mr and Mrs Grunt looked at each other then burst out laughing. "Help people? You do get some funny ideas sometimes, Sunny!" said Mr Grunt. "Now, go and hitch up creaky old Clip and Clop, will you? We have an appointment to keep."

That was the first Sunny had heard about any appointment. "We do?" he asked.

"We do." Mr Grunt nodded.

Sunny was trying to get the two donkeys

119

out of the cottage garden when Elsie Spawn, the elderly owner of the cottage – a very angry-looking woman with very blue hair – threw open her bedroom window and started shouting.

"Vandals!" she shouted. "Turnip-heads! Vagabonds! Hoodlums! Looters! Pillagers!" She was getting more and more purple in the face.

What Mr and Mrs Grunt and Sunny didn't know was that Elsie Spawn had been doing a crossword when she'd spotted Clip and Clop eating her lovely flowers. And, along with a sharp pencil (with a rubber on the end) and a nice cup of tea, there were two things Elsie Spawn always kept close to hand when doing a crossword: a dictionary and a thesaurus.

She used the *dictionary* to check the spelling of words she was trying to fit into the little

white squares. She used the *thesaurus* to find words with similar meanings to other words in the clues, because that's what it's there for. She quickly looked down the page of the thesaurus for more insults: "Mischief-makers! Plunderers! THIEVES!"

Mr Grunt had been merrily ignoring the insults raining down on Sunny as he led the donkeys back to the caravan, but he couldn't let the word THIEVES pass without action.

He stomped off the asphalt into the garden, trampling flowers as he went. "No, lady," he bellowed. "THIS is what *thieves* do!' He wrapped his arms round a pretty flowering bush and with one swift tug pulled the whole thing out of the ground. And using his poshest voice – the one that he usually saved for talking to judges in court – said, "I'll thank you to remember the difference." He began lugging the bush back to the caravan, fuming indignantly.

Elsie Spawn was aghast. She was agape; agog; dumbstruck; dumbfounded. (You get the picture.)

As well as the day's crossword, a nice sharp pencil, a cup of tea, a dictionary and a thesaurus, there was something *else* Elsie Spawn had readily to hand.

Perhaps I should have mentioned it earlier, but I have a lot to think about, you know. My shiny shoes don't polish themselves.

She had a blunderbuss loaded with black peppercorns.

Before you could say, "Ready! Take aim! Fire!", she'd lifted the firearm to the open window and pulled the trigger. There was a bang loud enough to wake a sleeping chicken, and an almost blinding flash followed by a cloud of soot-like smoke.

When the smoke cleared, Elsie Spawn's hair no longer looked blue, and Mr Grunt had dropped the bush and was dancing around in circles clutching the seat of his trousers with both hands, howling like someone who'd just been shot in the bottom with a hail of black peppercorns. Clip and Clop had been frightened by the sudden flash-bang-wallop, so bared their teeth, started "Hee-haw"-ing, and kicked the nearest thing, which happened to be Mrs Grunt. She went flying through the air, past her dancing husband, and – much to her utter amazement – landed in a seated position on the top step of the caravan.

Back in her bedroom,

meanwhile, Elsie Spawn was looking around for something to reload the blunderbuss with. She spotted a jar full of hairpins on her dressing table and quickly tipped the contents into her arthritic fingers, stuffing them down the trumpet-like end of the blunderbuss.

Soon she was ready to fire a second time, and thrust the nose of her weapon through the open window once more. Her face dropped in disappointment when she saw that the boy in the blue dress had managed to hitch up the donkeys and the blaggards/brutes/rascals were getting away!

She fired the blunderbuss just for the fun of it anyway, the lethal hairpins glinting in the fading light, like a flash of silvery fish darting through clear waters. They landed harmlessly in the garden, embedded in the lawn, flowerbeds and the trunks of trees.

The flash and the bang were less
harmless though: they caused
Elsie Spawn's once-blue hair
to catch alight.

She snatched a bedside jug of water and tipped it over her head. There was a hiss like frying bacon.

Elsie Spawn looked down on her damaged garden in dismay and at the bush lying in the middle of the lane. She then caught a glimpse of her reflection in her dressing-table mirror. She looked as if she'd been rolling in the ashes of a camp fire.

The elderly lady sighed. She didn't know their names but she certainly wouldn't forget the Grunts in a hurry. Whoever they were, they were nothing but *trouble*.

The appointment Mr Grunt had talked about was round the back of a dingy old barn about two hours' ride away by caravan. If the barn was dingy, round the back of it was dingier still. Mrs Grunt gave Sunny a large nettle-and-goat's-cheese roll and a bottle of home-made conker fizz, and Mr Grunt told him to wait round the back for a Mr Lippy.

"Don't talk to anyone else," he said.

"How will I know he's Mr Lippy?" said Sunny.

"Ask him his name," said Mrs Grunt.

"But if he turns out *not* to be Mr Lippy then I'll have talked to someone who isn't him, and Dad said—"

Mrs Grunt frowned. "You think too much,

Sunny," she said. "Bad for your brain. If you want to grow up smart like your dad, don't think so much."

"You'll know Mr Lippy is Mr Lippy when you see him," Mr Grunt assured the boy. "Now leave us be."

Sunny left Mr and Mrs Grunt in the caravan, huddled in front of the television set. The television was one of those old box-shaped ones – not a flat screen – but the actual telly part had been taken out long ago and replaced with a fish tank that fitted inside it perfectly.

Beautifully lit, the Grunts loved watching the handful of colourful fish dart around inside it, between plastic weeds. Mrs Grunt was always sure to stick her beloved Ginger Biscuit on the sofa between her and Mr Grunt, his glass eyes facing the little fishes.

The barn and surrounding field were used for everything from dances to amateur plays, fêtes to pig races, and dog shows to prize-vegetable competitions. All over the outer walls there were torn remains of posters announcing these various events, which had been pasted up, then pasted over with new ones, over the years.

As the summer evening light began to fade, Sunny found himself finishing off his roll and trying to make sense of the snatches of words: *FOR ONE OR TWO NIGHTS ONLY . . . back by fairly popular demand . . . CHILDREN*

ALMOST FREE . . . You Won't Believe Your Half-Closed Eyes . . . PAY AT DOOR OR SNEAK IN LATE . . . in its 3rd quite good year . . . Singing! Dancing! Falling Over! . . . Nearly All You Can Eat! There were also the names of various actors, singers and performers dotted among the shreds of poster, but one name seemed to leap out at him: *THE REMARKABLE CHINN TWINS*.

Where had he heard them mentioned before?

"Boo!" said a voice.

Sunny gave a little jump and turned to find himself face-to-face with a man with unnaturally curly hair and an *enormous* pair of bright-red lips. In the failing light, Sunny could see that his skin was a pale, chalky white.

Sunny suddenly felt nervous. Mr Grunt had told him that he'd know Mr Lippy was Mr

Lippy when he saw him, and here was a man with enormous lips. This could, of course, mean that the man's real name wasn't Mr Lippy but that he *called* himself Mr Lippy on account of his lips . . .

. . . the only problem was that if the man with the humongous lips *wasn't* Mr Lippy and Sunny asked him if he *was* Mr Lippy, he might not take too kindly to someone asking such an apparently rude question. And he might punch Sunny on the nose.

"Are you looking for a Mr L?" asked the man.

"Y-yes," said Sunny. "A Mr Lippy."

"Then you found him! I'm Lippy by name, Lippy by nature!" said the man in a sing-song tone that somehow suggested to Sunny that he'd said it a thousand times before.

Mr Lippy looked at Sunny closely, taking

in the sticky-up hair, the wonky ears – the left much higher than the right – and, of course, the blue dress. "Have you got something for me?" he asked.

"Er, no," said Sunny. "Am I supposed to have?"

"Are you sure you haven't been given something to give to me?"

"All Dad gave me was a nettle-and-goat's-cheese roll and a bottle of home-made conker fizz," said Sunny.

"Is that it?" asked Mr Lippy, pointing at an old Coke bottle filled with a rich, brown, gravy-thick liquid and stoppered with a small cork. It was propped up against the tree stump where Sunny had been sitting.

"Yup." Sunny nodded.

"Aren't you thirsty?" asked the big-lipped Mr Lippy.

"It's not because I'm not thirsty that I'm not drinking it," said Sunny, tying himself in "nots".

"Then why not?"

"Because it tastes disgusting," said Sunny.

"May I?" said Mr Lippy.

"Be my guest," said Sunny.

Mr Lippy bent down, put the neck of the bottle between his super-ginormous lips, pulled out the cork with them, spitting it into the grass, and then glugged down the conker fizz in one go. When he'd finished, he smacked his lips – and that was one BIG smack – then wiped them on his sleeve – with one BIG wipe.

"Ah!" said Mr Lippy. "You're absolutely right, son. That was truly horrible."

For a fleeting millisecond, Sunny wondered whether Mr Lippy had called him son because he was his real father, or because he was someone who called most boys son if he didn't know their names. As a reflex action, he found himself glancing down at the man's feet to see if he was wearing super-shiny black shoes (as he thought he remembered his father had worn). It turned out Mr Lippy was wearing shoes far bigger than any human being's feet could ever hope to be. And they were lime green.

Sunny suddenly had a thought. A good one. "Er – Mr Lippy?" he asked. "Are you by any chance a clown?"

"What on EARTH gave you that idea?" asked Mr Lippy, roaring with laughter. "My tight curly red hair? My lips painted bright red, my huge shoes, or my comedy squirty-flower?"

"What comedy squirty-flower?" asked Sunny.

Mr Lippy looked down at the lapel of his slightly threadbare mauve jacket. "Oh, botheration!" he snapped. "It must have

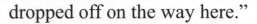

dropped off on the way here."

"Aren't you off duty?" asked Sunny, more than a little intrigued.

"How do you mean?" asked Mr Lippy.

"I mean, you're here to meet me, but you're still in—"

"My clowning clobber? Not all of it. I'm not in my comedy trousers and funny stretch braces. It's difficult to ride my bike when I've got them on."

"Isn't it difficult to cycle wearing those?" asked Sunny, looking down at the huge pair of lime-green shoes.

"Oh, not if I splay out my feet and pedal with my heels," said Mr Lippy. "And, anyway, I couldn't find my proper shoes. I think Trunk might have hidden them for a joke."

"Is Trunk a circus elephant?"

Mr Lippy shook his head. "No, no. Not him.

Don't let Trunk hear you call him that! He's a circus strongman. No neck to speak of. His body sort of ends and his head sort of begins with nothing in between."

"Oh," said Sunny (because he thought he should say something).

"But as much as I'd love to stay and chat, you're supposed to have something for me."

"Maybe Dad forgot. Would you mind waiting here?"

"As long as you're quick," said Mr Lippy.

Sunny dashed round to the front of the barn and down a small track, veering off across the field to a clump of trees behind which the Grunts had parked the caravan out of sight.

"Did you get it, Sunny?" asked Mr Grunt, eagerly looking up from the sofa.

"He seems to think we've got something to give him, not the other way around," said

Sunny.

Mr Grunt smacked himself in the middle of his forehead with the heel of his palm. "The envelope!" he said. "I forgot to give you the envelope. It's in the top drawer of the kitchen dresser."

Sunny went over to the dresser and pulled open the top drawer. On top of the usual mess of bits of string, bottle tops, takeaway menus and a single clothes peg was a sealed envelope. He pulled it out. "This one, Dad?" he asked.

"That's the one, Sunny," said Mr Grunt. "You go and give him that. There's a good lad." He turned his attention back to the fish in the television.

It was suddenly getting really dark now as Sunny made his way around the back of the barn. He was half expecting the clown not to be there, but Mr Lippy was sitting on the tree stump. "Got it?" he asked, rising to his (big-shoed) feet.

"Got it," said Sunny, handing him the envelope. "Though why Dad couldn't just give it to you himself . . ."

"Better this way," said Mr Lippy. "This way, if anyone asks, we can honestly say that he and I have never met and certainly didn't meet this evening."

"And why should anyone ask?" asked Sunny.

Mr Lippy handed him a similar-sized envelope in return. "Elephants often lead to lots of questions," said Mr Lippy.

TOP SECRIT FOR MISTUR LIPY

"Elephants?" said Sunny, but he

was talking to thin air. Mr Lippy was already climbing on to his bicycle. Moments later, the clown was pedalling off into the night.

Chapter Eight

On the Trail!

"It's a map," Mr Grunt explained, opening the envelope at the kitchen table, unfolding the piece of paper from inside it. Mrs Grunt and Sunny sat either side of him.

"Map?" asked Sunny excitedly.

"You heard your father," said Mrs Grunt. "M-O-P, map."

"That's a mop," snorted Mr Grunt.

"No it isn't," said Mrs Grunt. "I know a map when I see one. And anyhows, a mop wouldn't fit in an envelope that size!"

"M-O-P spells mop!" said Mr Grunt.

"Of course it does," said Mrs Grunt. "But that's got nothing to do with—"

Mr Grunt banged his fist on the table. "You just said 'M-O-P, map'," he said.

"Didn't," said Mrs Grunt (who secretly suspected she might have).

"Did," said Mr Grunt.

"Didn't!"

"Did!"

"Didn't!"

"Did!"

"Didn't!"

"Did!"

"Didn't!"

"Did! Did! Did!" said Mr Grunt.

While they were busy arguing, Sunny studied the hand-drawn map lying on the table. The most interesting part was where the big X was, next to what looked like a small wooden building. The other side of the X were two words: ELEPHANT HERE.

"Dad?" he asked.

"What?" asked Mr Grunt.

"Did we just buy an elephant?"

"No."

"No?"

"No, Sunny. *You* just bought an elephant," said Mr Grunt. "Nothing to do with me or your mother."

"If you say so," said Sunny.

"He did say so!" snorted Mrs Grunt. "I saw his lips move and everything."

"But it wasn't my money," said Sunny.

"Money?" said Mr Grunt (with a grunt). "Who said anything about money?"

"Sunny just did," said Mrs Grunt helpfully.

Mr Grunt glared at her.

"Well, if it wasn't money in the envelope, what was it then?" asked Sunny. "What else can you pay for a circus elephant with?"

"Ooooh," said Mrs Grunt. "So it's not just any old kind of elephant – it's a CIRCUS elephant. I had no idea."

"Of course you had no idea, wife," said Mr

Grunt. "Because this buying-of-an-elephant business was nothing to do with us, was it?"

"I thought you said—"

"WAS IT?" Mr Grunt glowered.

"Um . . . No. You're right, mister," said Mrs Grunt with genuine pride at her husband's scheming.

"I'm only guessing it's from a circus," said Sunny, "because you . . . we . . . I bought it off Mr Lippy, who is a *clown*."

"We have taught you well, Sunny!" said Mr Grunt.

"What was in the envelope, if it wasn't money, Dad?"

"Another map, drawn by *me* this time," said Mr Grunt triumphantly.

"A map leading to something Mr Lippy wants?" asked Sunny. "So it's a sort of swap?"

"S'what he just said!" said Mrs Grunt.

"Kind of," said Mr Grunt.

"Why only 'kind of', Dad?" asked Sunny. He had an uneasy feeling in the pit of his stomach.

"Because although my map is real, what it leads to isn't *exactly* what I'd promised it would be," said Mr Grunt.

Now Sunny was feeling really uneasy. "What did you promise to give him in exchange for the elephant?" he asked.

"It doesn't matter, because what he's actually getting is close enough. Just not *precisely* what we agreed!" Mr Grunt laughed.

"Exactly!" said Mrs Grunt, who spent much of the time not really knowing what was going on but doing her best to pretend she did.

"But that's cheating!" said Sunny. "That's wrong."

"I'll tell you what's wrong, Sunny," said Mr

Grunt. "Stealing an elephant from a circus is what's wrong. Do you really think the elephant was Mr Lippy's to swap in the first place?"

"Not necessarily—"

"So you could argue that we're –" Mr Grunt tried to think of the right words. "We're teaching him a lesson."

"A lesson that you should never trust people!" said Mrs Grunt proudly.

"Quiet, wife," said Mr Grunt. "You're making a fool of yourself."

"No more than you are!" Mrs Grunt retorted.

"Numbskull!" said Mr Grunt.

"Toolbag!" said Mrs Grunt.

"Armpit!" said Mr Grunt.

"Trench coat!" said Mrs Grunt.

"Don't you think Mr Lippy will come looking for us when he finds out he's been tricked?" Sunny interrupted.

"He may not even notice. And if he does, we'll be long gone from here by then," said Mr Grunt.

"But circuses travel around too, and surely we won't be that hard to find," said Sunny.

"Why not?" said Mr Grunt.

"Because we'll have a hulking great elephant with us," said Sunny.

Mr Grunt was about to say something, but stopped. He looked flummoxed. He didn't have an answer to that.

The following morning – after a night in which both Mr and Mrs Grunt slept beautifully in their bed, and Sunny lay awake for much of it outside their door with a mixture of worry and excitement – the Grunts actually set off for a particular destination for the second time in two days.

Sunny was used to hitching up Clip and Clop and simply going where the donkeys and the Grunts' moods might lead them. Today, however, they were following Mr Lippy's map to collect *an elephant*.

Mr Grunt had given Sunny the task of reading the map and making sure that they were going the right way. He didn't trust Mrs Grunt to be able to do it, and had "important things" to do himself, apparently.

Sunny certainly heard much hammering, crashing and bashing, along with the occasional cry of pain when Mr Grunt must

have hit himself by mistake.

The clown's map wasn't particularly detailed but what details he had drawn were very useful. He'd shown landmarks to look out for (linked together by dotted lines and arrows), with instructions for what to do – turn left, straight on, turn right, etc. – once they were reached. (So it wasn't really a *proper* map. It was not to scale, with places in the right place or anything.)

The starting point was the old barn and the next landmark Sunny had to look out for as he led Clip and Clop westward was a crossroads by a windmill, where they'd have to turn right. They stopped briefly at the mill to give Mr and Mrs Grunt time to laugh and point at the miller in his flour-covered smock, and for Mr Grunt to kick one of the sacks of grain stacked at the roadside. (Mrs Grunt usually liked to

save her kicking-of-things for extra-special occasions.) They then hopped back inside the caravan, ready for Sunny to negotiate the bend.

It was quite a tight turn for the Grunts' extraordinarily higgledy-piggledy house on wheels. The roads were narrow, and the one he was supposed to be taking them down had high hedges on both sides. Sunny had to manoeuvre the caravan backwards and forwards quite a few times (which wasn't the easiest thing in the world when working with donkeys, especially ones that weren't quite as young as they used to be). Sunny talked to Clip and Clop, gently coaxing and praising them, and promising them juicy carrots in the not too distant future. He also gave them hearty pats on the haunches, stroked their muzzles and, when he *really* needed the pair to go beyond the call of donkey duty, scratched them between the ears. The Grunts' home was a big haul for Clip and Clop, even though there were actually two of them.

After the windmill crossroads, Sunny had to look out for a left-hand turn just after crossing a three-arched bridge, and a right-hand fork in the road next to a waterfall. He found these, along with the entrance to a shortcut by a fallen tree and a turning by a statue of a white stag – a deer with antlers – into a forest. The statue had recently been given a fresh coat of white gloss paint, so looked very shiny and unrealistic.

Sunny enjoyed following the map instructions: seeing places first as black-and-white drawings on paper, and later as the real thing. He liked being on the move with a purpose – and such an exciting purpose . . .

He found himself thinking of Mimi, imagining her not as he'd last seen her (in Sack the gardener's borrowed overalls) but as he'd first caught sight of her before the bee attack, at her very pinkest, when she was still smelling of roses, with the pink ribbon proudly tied in her hair. She'd said that she liked animals and she'd like to travel. And what was he doing right there and then? Travelling with two donkeys on his way to collect an elephant! It would have been great if she could have come too.

Thinking about Mimi made him think of Bigg Manor and of Larry Smalls hanging from the gate. And then – *bam!* – he remembered where he'd heard mention of the Chinn Twins before he'd read their name on the remains of a poster on the barn wall. Larry Smalls had said that if only *the Chinn Twins* had been there, they'd have been able to get him down from the gate easily (or something like that).

Maybe they were acrobats? On the poster they'd been referred to as being "remarkable". Sunny imagined one identical twin leaping up on to the back of the other and unhooking Larry Smalls from the top of the gates to Bigg Manor in one swift, graceful movement. What a sight that would have been!

After ten minutes or so of clip-clopping down the forest track, Clip and Clop decided that it was lunchtime, and they stopped. Sunny knew that there'd be no point in trying to make them go any further until they'd rested and eaten. And anyway, he was hungry too.

Mrs Grunt threw open an upstairs window. "Why have we stopped?" she demanded.

"Lunchtime," said Sunny.

Now *Mr* Grunt threw open a downstairs window. "Why have we stopped?" he demanded.

"Lunchtime," said Mrs Grunt.

"Good!" said Mr Grunt. "Make me an omelette, wife!" He pulled in his head and slammed the window shut.

"Make it yourself, mister!" shouted Mrs Grunt, slamming her window too.

In the end, Mr Grunt gathered some old fir cones from the forest floor while Sunny fed Clip and Clop. Mr Grunt then tossed the cones into a blender, ready to make some woody soup or other. Unfortunately, he forgot to put the lid on, and bits of fir cone shot around the kitchen like pieces of shrapnel. Mrs Grunt screamed and dived under the kitchen table, letting out an even BIGGER scream when she landed on Sharpie, the stuffed hedgehog.

"What's Sharpie doing under here?!" she yelped the moment Mr Grunt had fumbled with the off switch of the blender, and all was quiet.

"Not a lot, I expect," said Mr Grunt. "He's dead."

"I mean, who put him here?" said Mrs Grunt, rubbing her arm where the spines had gone in.

"Then say what you mean, wife!" Mr Grunt grunted.

"I just did," said Mrs Grunt.

"Oh, well done!" said Mr Grunt. "Do you want a medal?"

"Yes."

"Well, I can't make you one because I'm too busy *making lunch because my wife is too lazy to do it*," said Mr Grunt with enough menace in his voice to frighten the weevils in the cheese. (To be fair, though, cheese weevils are easily frightened, or so I've heard.)

"Too busy shooting chunks of fir cone about the place, more like!" said Mrs Grunt. "And I still want to know why you put Sharpie under the table."

"What makes you think it was me, wife?"

"Well, I didn't do it, and Sharpie's dead, so he can't have walked there by himself . . . so that leaves you, mister!" said Mrs Grunt.

"What about Sunny?"

Mrs Grunt gave a puzzled frown. "He's not dead," she snapped.

"I mean, who's to say that *Sunny* didn't move him?" said Mr Grunt.

"Because Sunny isn't an idiot," said Mrs Grunt.

Mr Grunt slammed the lid on the top of the blender, trapping what remained of the fir cones. "Are you saying that I am?" he demanded.

"That you are what?"

"An idiot!"

"Are you call me an idiot?" Mrs Grunt bristled.

"I was calling *me* an idiot!" said Mr Grunt. "No, I mean, I was asking to know whether *you* were calling me an idiot."

159

"Work it out for yourself," said Mrs Grunt, adding the words "you idiot" under her breath. They were drowned out by the noise of the blender when Mr Grunt hit the on switch again.

Chapter Nine

One Rung at a Time

It was with only a slight tummy ache that Sunny set Clip and Clop off again along the track after lunch. It was late afternoon when they left the forest, the trees as close together at the fringes as in its very heart.

Because of the nature of the map – it only showing landmarks to guide them by, leaving out everything else in between – it was impossible to gauge time and distances. On the map, for example, the distance between a blue house they'd had to turn right at and a tunnel they'd had to pass through was the same (on paper) as the distance between the windmill and the three-arched bridge. But on the ground, it took hours longer to get from house to tunnel.

Once out of the forest and following the road to the right (which was east), Sunny was on the lookout for what looked on the map like a large column with a statue on top. That should be easy enough to spot, he thought. And easy enough as it was – for reasons that will soon become clear – it looked rather different from the picture. There was something like a lay-by – a parking place and resting spot – at the side of the road, where the side of the hill behind had been carved out into a semicircle, with a low stone wall running along the base. In the middle of this area was the impressive column, which was about twenty metres tall.

Sunny led the donkeys into the lay-by, and stood and looked up at the statue on top of the column. It was of a man with side-whiskers and a big top hat. He appeared to be holding a giant bunch of wilted flowers in his right hand. Unlike the column, statue and surrounding wall – which were all obviously made of stone – the wilting flower-like-thingummies were made of some kind of metal. Only they weren't supposed to be flowers, of course. This was a statue of one of the early Lord Biggs, proudly clutching a handful of his railings, and they had wilted ten years and a week after they'd been made.

Sunny wasn't familiar with how the Bigg family had made their fortune, so might not have known this was a statue of one of the Biggs if it weren't for three things.

Firstly, the statue of this particular Lord

Bigg looked extraordinarily like the Lord Bigg he'd come face-to-face with in Sack's potting shed back at Bigg Manor (though it didn't have little stone sticking-plaster crosses all over its stone face).

Secondly, there was a big plaque screwed into the base of the column, which read: "LORD BIGG: He Made Our Cliff Tops Safe". (Well, what it actually said was: "LORD BIGG: He Mad Our li   ps Safe", because some of the letters had worn away.)

And thirdly, dotted all around the semicircle of the lay-by were handwritten placards that read: "BIGG AIN'T BEST". One placard was even tied round the statue's neck with old blue nylon rope. The statue's stone hat was also partially covered by an orange-and-white traffic cone, which had been plonked on top of it at a jaunty angle.

"Mr Smalls," said Sunny to himself, a slight smile appearing on his lips. He couldn't help having a sneaking admiration for the man (in much the same way that Larry Smalls had had a sneaking admiration for Lord Bigg when he mistakenly thought that he was the ex-boxer Barney "The Bruiser" Brown).

"What?" said Mr Grunt, tumbling out of the caravan. When he picked himself up, he found himself looking up at the statue with the traffic cone headgear. "Who's the wizard?" he asked.

"Lord Bigg," said Sunny. "Not the latest Lord Bigg. Not the one I met, but another one."

Mr Grunt looked at him blankly. He had *no* idea what the boy was on about. "We'll stop here for the night," he announced. "Tomorrow we collect Fingers."

"Fingers?" asked Sunny.

"Fingers." Mr Grunt nodded.

"Fingers?" asked Sunny. Again.

"The elephant," said Mr Grunt.

"That's a funny name for an elephant," said Sunny.

"Know many elephants, do you?" asked Mr Grunt, pleased with himself for his quick thinking and clever comment.

"Aren't they usually called Jumbo, or, er . . .?" Sunny couldn't think of any elephant names other than Jumbo, so he stopped there.

Very little traffic passed that way that night, and even Sunny slept soundly until he was awoken by the pop-pop-pop of a passing motorcycle at around three o'clock in the morning. Luckily, he managed to get back to sleep.

First up, Sunny went outside to see what

Clip and Clop were up to (which turned out to be chewing things), only to come face-to-face with a middle-aged man with snow-white hair, a yellow checked waistcoat and an arm in plaster.

"Mornin'," said the man. "You've gotta be Sunny!"

"How do you mean?" asked Sunny.

"The way Mimi described your mobile home and your – er – blue dress an' that," said the man, finding it difficult to take his eyes off Sunny's head, with his sticky-up hair and wonky ears (which were probably something else Mimi had mentioned).

"You know Mimi?" asked Sunny. The world somehow felt that bit sunnier to Sunny, simply at the mention of her name.

"Know her?" said the man. "I taught her everything she needed to know to become an excellent boot boy." He put out a bandaged hand. (The one on the end of the arm that wasn't in a plaster cast.) "I'm Jack the handyman," he said, grasping Sunny's hand, "also known as Handyman Jack."

"You work at Bigg Manor?" Sunny asked.

"Yes. I used to be boot boy until Mimi took

over," he explained.

"So what brings you this far?" asked Sunny.

"Far?" said Jack, raising a snow-white eyebrow. "If you carry on down this road another half-mile and take a right, you'll find yourself on the edge of the Bigg estate."

"Oh," said Sunny. The map had given no suggestion of that. They must have been going around in circles.

"I've been instructed to clear up this mess," said Jack, looking around at the "BIGG AIN'T BEST"'s dotted all over the place.

"I see you brought a ladder," said Sunny, looking at Jack the handyman's vehicle. It was an adult-sized black-framed tricycle with a matching black metal trailer attached to the back, with a large number of ladders either side and a heap of tools in the middle.

"I certainly came prepared," said Jack.

"Would you like a hand?" asked Sunny, looking at the bandage and the plaster cast. "I don't think they'll be awake for a while." He jerked his head in the direction of the caravan.

Jack tilted his whole body back to look to the very top of the column. "I could do with someone holding the ladder when I go up there," he said.

"I'd be happy to," said Sunny.

Handyman Jack had to fit all the ladders together to make one long one to reach all the way up to the statue. He slipped them into position quickly and efficiently (despite the plastered arm and bandaged hand), but Sunny still felt a little doubtful.

"Will that be safe?" he asked.

"You sound like my wife," said the handyman, referring to Agnes, the cook and maid back at Bigg Manor. "It'll be a lot safer than if you weren't holding it for me, that's for sure!"

Sunny gripped the sides of the ladder and gave it a shake. The top, some twenty or so metres above them, wibbled and wobbled (though I'm not absolutely sure "wibbled" is a real word).

"Here I go!" said Jack. "That Larry Smalls has a lot to answer for! If I break my neck, there's only him to blame!" He sounded very cheerful about it. When Jack's feet were on the fifth or sixth rung – level with Sunny's eyes – the boy found himself staring at the shiniest pair of black lace-up shoes he'd ever seen.

Shiny black shoes.

He also noticed that Jack was wearing one spotted sock and one plain. He found his thoughts returning to his one memory of his father.

"Jack?" he called up, almost afraid of the answer before he'd even asked the question.

"Yes, Sunny?" Jack called back down.

"Do you have any children?"

"No," said Jack.

No? thought Sunny. *Oh*, thought Sunny. Then another thought occurred to him. "Did you ever lose any?" he asked.

"I'm sorry?"

"I mean, I know you just said you don't have any children but I was wondering if you meant that you don't have any children *now*. That you might have had one once and – er – lost it," said Sunny.

"Oh, like His Lordship, you mean?" asked

173

Jack. "No."

Like His Lordship?

"What's that about Lord Bigg?" asked Sunny, tightening his grip on the ladder, making his knuckles whiten.

Jack kept on climbing as he talked. "He and Lady Bigg had a son but they mislaid him years ago. They can't remember where they put him," said Jack.

"How old is he?" asked Sunny.

Jack stopped. He'd now reached the halfway point, about fifteen metres above the ground. "Er, I suppose he must be about your age," he said.

Sunny suddenly had a funny feeling in his tummy, and he was sure that it was nothing to do with the fir-cone soup this time. He simply stood there in silence, holding the ladder, while Jack reached the top and then

174

somehow managed to knock the orange-and-white traffic cone off the statue's stone hat – "Watch out below!" – and cut the blue nylon rope off the placard around the statue's neck. This done, he tossed the placard to the ground.

Caught in a tiny eddy of air, it spun over to the Grunts' caravan and landed on its roof, before skittering to the ground with a thwack. As Jack made his way back down the ladder, Sunny spoke again. "What's Lord Bigg's son's name?" he asked.

"Horace," said Jack.

"You remember him?"

"Course I do. My wife, Agnes, used to look after him sometimes. Wash him. Change him. Sing to him."

Just as Handyman Jack said the words "sing to him", his shiny shoes had reached Sunny's eye level again.

"Sing to him?"

"Oh yes, my Agnes has the voice of an angel. She could sing you the list of anti-allergy pills and medicines she has to take, and it would sound beautiful."

A man with shiny shoes.

A woman with the voice of an angel.

What if these memories weren't of his actual mother and father, but memories of SERVANTS of his mother and father's? What if he was the missing son of Lord and Lady Bigg!?!

Just behind Sunny came a belch loud enough to frighten the beetles in the undergrowth.

There was a familiar smell of pickling vinegar and open drains.

"Pardon!" said Mrs Grunt with such glee that it was obvious she didn't mean it. "Where did you get that ladder from, Sunny?" she asked. "It's the longest I've ever seen." She peered at it more closely. "Did you know that there's a funny little white-haired man attached to it?"

"This is Handyman Jack from Bigg Manor," said Sunny. "Or Jack the handyman."

"Make your mind up!" snapped Mrs Grunt.

"He's both," Sunny explained. "It's his ladder."

"Pity," said Mrs Grunt. "You can never go wrong with a good ladder."

Jack took the final few rungs to the ground.

"Pleased to meet you, ma'am," he said.

"Pleased to meet her?" bellowed Mr Grunt, emerging from the caravan. "Then you obviously don't know her!" He snorted with delight at his witty repartee. "The woman is nothing but walking trouble."

Mrs Grunt went off foraging for food for breakfast (returning later with a basketful of what she called "mushrooms" but which Mr

Grunt informed her were "highly poisonous toadstools". She went on to insist that they were perfectly fine to eat and that her cousin

Lil had regularly eaten mushrooms *just like them*. When Mr Grunt asked which one of her many cousins Cousin Lil was, Mrs Grunt replied, "The one who died from poisoning.").

Sunny, meanwhile, took the opportunity to ask Handyman Jack more about Horace.

"What did he look like?" he asked.

"Why the interest?" said Jack, who was busy gathering up the remaining BIGG AIN'T BEST placards.

"Oh, I just wondered," said Sunny unconvincingly.

"He was little more than a baby," said Jack. "And between you and me –" He lowered his voice and leaned in close – "all babies look pretty much alike to me."

"Oh," said Sunny. "No birthmark or anything?"

"Distinguishing features?" said Handyman

Jack, rubbing his chin. "No, not really. Apart from his ears."

HIS EARS?!?

"His ears?" asked Sunny.

"Yup." Jack nodded. "He had three of them."

Sunny's jaw dropped.

"Only jokin'!" said Jack with a loud guffaw. "He only had two of 'em and they were perfectly normal."

Sunny's heart sank. "Unlike mine," he said, barely above a whisper.

"There's nothing wrong with your ears, Sunny!" said the handyman cheerily.

Sunny rather suspected he was just saying that to be nice.

Chapter Ten

Round, Round, Get Around!

Soon the column and Handyman Jack were far behind Sunny, Mr and Mrs Grunt, and Clip and Clop as their journey in search of Fingers the elephant entered its final phase.

One of the pictures on Mr Lippy the clown's map-that-wasn't-quite-a-map was what appeared to be a giant tomato at the side of the road. Ever since Sunny had first seen it, he'd been looking forward to finding out what it was for real and now here it was . . .

. . . and it appeared to be just that: a giant

tomato. Not big as in "Cor! That's a big 'un! How did you grow that?" but big as in BIG ENOUGH TO LIVE IN.

Sunny stopped the caravan and walked over to it. Even close up it looked incredibly lifelike. He gave it a tap; it sounded hollow.

"Fibreglass," said Mr Grunt, leaning out of an upstairs window. "I'll bet it's fibreglass."

"What do you reckon it's *for*, Dad?" asked Sunny.

"Dunno," said Mr Grunt with a grunt. He came out of the caravan and gave the giant pretend fruit – tomatoes aren't vegetables, you know – a good kick. (Or, I should say, a *bad* kick, because one shouldn't go kicking things, apart from footballs and the like, and even then only when you're supposed to.)

The kick had an immediate effect. A very small man appeared from the other side of the

tomato and without so much as a word kicked
Mr Grunt very hard in the shins.

This was so unexpected, and so painful, that
Mr Grunt not only fell to the ground like a ton
of turnips but he also burst into tears. This was
enough to bring Mrs Grunt on to the scene to
find out what all the fuss was about.

"What's this fuss all about?" she demanded.

"He kicked me!" Mr Grunt managed to say between sobs and gulps of air.

"He kicked my tomato first!" said the small man.

"That's true," said Sunny, who was helping Mr Grunt to his feet.

"Which is true?" asked Mrs Grunt.

"They're both telling the truth," said Sunny.

Mrs Grunt glared at her husband. "You can't go kicking other people's tomatoes and expect to get away with it," she said, swinging back her leg and giving the giant fibreglass tomato an almighty kick. (See? I said she saved her kicks for special occasions, and what occasion could be more special than one where she could kick the tomato of someone who'd just kicked her lovely husband?)

"Stop it!" cried the man. "Please stop it! You'll break it!"

"Oh, boo-hoo!" said Mrs Grunt. "You shouldn't go kicking my husband then, should you?"

"Why doesn't everyone stop kicking everyone and everything else?" said Sunny. "Just a suggestion."

"And a good one," said Mr Grunt, who'd stopped blubbing now. "And I wasn't crying, by the way. I had something in my eye."

"Yeah," said Mrs Grunt. "Tears from crying."

"Didn't you just hear what I said, wife? I said—"

"I'm Sunny," said Sunny, putting his hand out for the little man to shake. The man shook it.

"I'm Jeremy," he said.

"What's this tomato doing here?" asked Sunny, who was dying to know. It was so big.

And so shiny and red, glinting in the afternoon sunshine. It appeared to have been lovingly polished.

"It was used in a TV advertisement for a tomato sauce a few years back," said Jeremy, "and when they didn't need it any more I offered to buy it from them."

"Wow," said Sunny.

"And in the end they actually gave it to me for nothing as long as I arranged to have it taken away," said Jeremy.

"What do you use it for?" asked Sunny.

"Use it for?" asked Jeremy.

"I mean, it looks great, but I wonder if you got it for a particular purpose?" said Sunny.

"I got it for a *very* particular purpose," said Jeremy. "I live in it."

"Oh," said Sunny. He hadn't been expecting that.

"It's boiling hot in the summer and freezing cold in the winter," said Jeremy.

"Is that a good thing?"

"No. That's a terrible thing. And stuffy. Look." Jeremy led Sunny round to the other side of the tomato, where there was a proper door. "I had this door put in, but decided that adding windows would stop it looking like a tomato, so I didn't."

"Didn't?"

"Add any."

"Oh," said Sunny. "Why do you live in a tomato?" he asked, trying to sound as polite as possible.

Jeremy looked over to the Grunts' caravan. "Is that your home?" he asked.

"Yes." Sunny nodded.

The little man shrugged. "Well, we've all gotta live somewhere," he said. He caught sight of Mr Lippy's map in Sunny's hand. "What's that?" he asked.

Mr Grunt, who'd obviously overheard the question, appeared at his side. "That," he said, snatching the map from Sunny's grasp, "is none of your business. That's what that is. Put it away, Sunny," he said, handing it back to the boy. "Keep it away from prying eyes." He glared at Jeremy.

Sunny folded the map and stuffed it in the pocket in his blue dress.

"It looked like Mr Lippy's writing, that's all," said Jeremy.

"You know Mr Lippy?" asked Sunny.

"We, on the other hand, have never heard of him," said Mr Grunt. He gave Sunny a stare. "Who is he?"

"Just some clown," said Jeremy, "with handwriting just like that." He pointed at the top of the map sticking out from Sunny's pocket.

"Well," said Mr Grunt. "We must be going." He appeared to be walking away, then suddenly turned and ran towards Jeremy to give him a get-his-own-back kick . . .

. . . but Jeremy was too fast and neatly stepped to one side at the very last moment, like a matador teasing a bull.

When Mr Grunt's foot failed to come into contact with a person as planned, it kept on moving, causing him to fall to the ground a second time – not that anyone was counting – with an "UMPFF!".

Mrs Grunt simply stepped over him. "Stop lying around, mister," she said. "We've an elephant to find."

"Keep your voice down, idiot wife!" he hissed through gritted teeth.

But if Jeremy had heard her mention an elephant, he didn't let it show. He slammed the front door – the *only* door – of the tomato behind him as he went inside.

"Charming!" said Mr Grunt, now upright. He turned to Mrs Grunt. "Wife, no more blabbering about a certain E-L-I-F-A-N-T." Next, he turned to Sunny. "And you keep your lips closed about knowing Mr Lippy," he reminded him.

"Sorry, Dad," said Sunny.

Sunny gave him a slap on the back. "No harm done," he said.

The rest of the trek to reach Fingers was uneventful. Sunny led them to the right when he reached the crooked house; took the twisty, almost-back-on-yourself left at the rock shaped like a toad; and finally led them down the path to the barn.

Not *a* barn. *The* barn. The barn where they'd started out from. Of course, this barn was drawn in a completely different place on the map because – remember – it wasn't really a proper map with everything in its place relative to everything else. It was more an illustrated list of instructions, showing landmarks and where to turn. So on the piece of paper there were TWO barns. The one showing where to start from – where Mr Lippy and Sunny had met – and this barn, which was shown as being NOWHERE NEAR that one . . . Only, in real life, it was one and the same.

Sunny had a sinking feeling as they approached.

"Dad!" he called out. "Good news and bad news."

Mr Grunt opened the top of the stable-like door. "What is it?" he asked.

"We're nearly there."

"That's the good news?"

"Yes, Dad."

"What's the bad news?" Mrs Grunt demanded, pushing Mr Grunt aside, and sitting her sawdust-filled doorstop, Ginger Biscuit, on the top of the bottom half of the door, for a better view.

"We're back at the barn we started from."

"That doesn't matter so long as there's an elephant inside," said Mrs Grunt.

"It might be bad news, if Mr Lippy brought along the elephant," said Sunny.

"Why's that, Sunny?" asked Mr Grunt, elbowing his wife out of the way. Ginger Biscuit nearly toppled off, but Mrs Grunt managed to catch him by the tail.

"Because you gave him a map that led him to something which – according to you – isn't quite what you promised it would be."

"Oh, that," said Mr Grunt. "Yes, that *is* bad news." He didn't sound too bothered.

"So what do you want me to do?" asked Sunny.

"Do? Keep going till we reach the barn," said Mr Grunt.

"Yes," said Mrs Grunt. "Get on with it!" Now both of them were crammed in the doorway.

"You never know," said Mr Grunt. "We may have luck on our side!"

Since when had the Grunts EVER had luck

on their side, Sunny wondered, but he didn't say anything.

In next to no time he'd pulled up near the barn with a mixture of excitement and dread.

Chapter Eleven

Fingers

It probably comes as no great surprise for you to learn that Mr and Mrs Grunt decided Sunny should be the one to go into the barn. There was no sign of life outside so, if there was going to be any elephant action, or funny business – there was potential clown involvement here, remember – it was likely to occur behind those two mighty closed doors.

Mr Grunt insisted that they hide the caravan behind the trees as before, though it being broad daylight and their having had to cross an open field, it was unlikely that anyone on the lookout would have failed to spot them.

"Good luck, Sunny," said Mr Grunt.

"Be brave," said Mrs Grunt, "and leave your shoes behind, will you? It'd be a shame to waste them."

"Waste them?"

"Your mother means in case you don't come back," Mr Grunt explained.

Sunny didn't bother arguing. He kicked off his non-matching shoes – one slip-on and one blue-laced lace-up – and felt the grass between his toes. "What is it exactly that you want me to do?" he asked.

"Be friendly. If it's Mr Lippy, smile as

though you haven't a care in the world. If it's someone else, simply say that you're here for the – er – elephant."

"And if whoever-it-may-be asks about the stuff you gave him not being the stuff you promised?"

"Protest your innocence!" said Mr Grunt, using the very piece of advice his lawyer had given him the time he was arrested for stealing a statue carved from Cheddar cheese. (Fortunately for him, some hungry mice ate the evidence before there could be a trial. Mrs Grunt had bribed the mice to do it. She'd promised them as much cheese as they could eat.)

"Stand firm!" said Mrs Grunt.

"And if things turn nasty?" asked Sunny.

"Then run like Billy-o!" said Mrs Grunt.

"Billy-o?" asked Sunny.

Mrs Grunt shrugged. "I think Billy-o must have been a really fast runner," she said. ("Running like Billy-o" was simply a phrase her own mother had used and – like you and Sunny – she had no idea what it really meant.)

"Did he run in bare feet?" asked Sunny.

Neither Mr nor Mrs Grunt said anything. Mrs Grunt had spotted a dead crow and her thoughts were turning to an early supper.

Sunny had a quiet word with Clip and Clop, patting their muzzles and scratching them between the ears, then headed off to the barn.

Though huge, the right-hand door to the barn was unlocked, and swung open surprisingly easily. Sunny stepped nervously inside. Sunlight poured through some of the gaps between the planks in the walls, or the holes where there had once been knots in the wood, but much of the inside of the barn was in shadow.

Fingers, however, was easy enough to spot.

It's hard to hide an elephant, even in a big barn.

"You!" said a surprised voice.

It was a familiar voice too. But it didn't belong to Mr Lippy. It was a voice that Sunny was more used to hearing say, "BIGG AIN'T BEST."

"Mr Smalls!" he said. "What are you doing here?"

"Sitting on an elephant," said Larry Smalls. Now that Sunny had become more accustomed to the light, he could indeed see Mr Smalls astride the elephant. And what a lovely-looking elephant he was too. All friendly.

"What about you?"

"What about me, Mr Smalls?"

"What are YOU doing here?"

"I've come to collect the elephant," said Sunny.

Larry Smalls smiled. He actually smiled. This was probably the first time Sunny had seen Larry Smalls smile and the transformation was amazing. He looked like a different man. He didn't look like a man with a grudge who spent his time writing placards and throwing rocks and being all bitter about Lord Bigg. He looked *happy*.

"You? You're the mystery buyer?"

"Kind of," said Sunny.

"It makes perfect sense, I suppose," said Larry Smalls, sliding off the side of Fingers on to one of a number of bales of hay that had been lined up in rows to form seats (for an upcoming play).

"It does?" said Sunny, surprised.

"Of course!" said Mr Smalls. "I was wondering who'd want to buy an elephant, apart from a circus or zoo or wildlife park, I mean. Having seen the size of your – er – caravan, though, it makes perfect sense!"

"You think Dad's bought him to take over from Clip and Clop?"

"The two donkeys?" asked Larry Smalls.

Sunny nodded.

"An elephant would find the job a whole lot easier!" said Smalls.

Sunny smiled. He could just imagine Fingers pulling along their home as easy as pie. Then his face fell. What would happen to Clip and Clop? Would the Grunts simply abandon them now that they didn't need them? Hadn't he heard Mr Grunt grumbling about them getting old and not wanting to do the donkey work any more? A little knot of worry formed in the pit of his stomach. Sunny suddenly realised just how much he loved the big-eared pair.

"Won't Fingers mind lugging a great big house around?" he asked.

"Mind? He'll love it," said Larry Smalls rummaging in his pocket and pulling out a fist full of peanuts (still in their shells). Fingers' trunk swung into action, snuffling them up surprisingly elegantly and putting them in his mouth, all the while watching them with his highly intelligent eyes.

"I rescued Fingers from a rich animal collector when he was a baby," Mr Smalls explained. "You see, I never took animals from the wild. That would be wrong. He was chained up in a tiny cage, but with me he's had a life on the open road!

He'd pull the circus trucks. Help erect the tent poles for the big top."

"You used to work in a circus?"

"I used to *own* a circus," said Larry Smalls. "Smalls' Big Top. All our animals had been rescued in some way or other."

"But isn't it cruel to make them do tricks?"

"Not the way I did it," said Smalls. "We let the animals find their own talents. Why make a sea lion balance a ball on his nose if he prefers doing card tricks? Why make a lion jump through a hoop when he might prefer to hold a brush in his mouth and do a little painting?"

Fingers wasn't waiting for Larry Smalls to give him more peanuts. He put his trunk directly into the man's other pocket and pulled out some for himself.

"So what happened?" asked Sunny.

"What do you mean?" asked Larry Smalls.

"What happened to Smalls' Big Top?"

Larry Smalls' face passed into the shadows. "Lord Bigg is what happened," he said. "Him and his railings."

At the mention of Bigg's name, Fingers stopped chewing.

"I don't understand," said Sunny.

"Then let me explain," said Larry Smalls. "Sit."

Sunny made himself as comfortable as he could on a nearby bale of straw.

"People often think that fences around enclosures and bars on cages are there to protect people from animals and, of course, that's partly true," said Larry Smalls. "But they're also there to protect the animals from the people. You see, stupid people do stupid things. They try to feed animals the wrong

kinds of food. They prod them when they're sleeping. They flash cameras in their faces. The tease them. Upset them." Smalls himself looked upset at the thought of this, and paused for a moment. "So bars work both ways. And the metal bars – the metal railings – we used for our cages when the animals were on the move, and for the enclosures when we were camped, were made by the Bigg Railing Company."

"Lord Bigg makes railings?" asked Sunny.

"Used to," said Smalls, and he told Sunny *all* about it, pretty much as I told you many, many chapters ago (though probably not quite so well as I did, what with my being such a brilliant author).

"So did the railings on your cages go floppy after ten years and a week?" Sunny gasped.

"Yes," said Larry Smalls. "We had no idea

that was going to happen, of course. One night we went to bed with all the animals safe and sound. The next morning, disaster! In the night the bars had gone floppy, the animals wandered out and . . . and . . ."

"And?" Sunny leaned forward on his straw bale.

"We'd pitched the circus in a field as part of a steam tractor festival. There were huge-great steam-powered machines everywhere . . . including steam*rollers* . . ."

"You mean, the animals . . .?"

Larry Smalls nodded. "Many of them were as flat as pancakes."

Sunny imagined a squashed lion in the middle of the road. How terrible! Then he couldn't help himself. He imagined Mr and Mrs Grunt shovelling it up between them and making a casserole. He could picture the tail sticking out of the cooking pot.

"No wonder you hate Lord Bigg!" said
Sunny. "I'm so sorry, Mr Smalls."

"Thank you, Sunny," said Larry Smalls. "I
knew you were a good kid from the moment

you – er – kind of caught me."

Sunny felt like a fraudster and a cheat, remembering that the "payment" for Fingers wasn't what Larry Smalls would be expecting. He tried not to think about it. "So what happened to the rest of the circus?" he asked.

"Mr Lippy, who you met, does children's parties, and he runs the odd errand for me. The Chinn Twins – my acrobats – trim treetops and repair telephone lines. Sammy the sea lion works in a call centre—"

"A call centre?"

"Yes, when people complain to one of the telephone operators and demand to speak to their supervisor, he barks down the phone at them. Most effective, apparently."

Mr Smalls then went on to list some of the others in their new roles, including Trunk the strongman, who had opened a specialist shirt shop for men with no neck to speak of, and Jeremy the juggler, who now lived in a large fibreglass fruit.

"So Fingers is the only animal you have left?" said Sunny.

"Yes," said Smalls. He probably wasn't even aware of it, but he was gently stroking the elephant's trunk as he spoke. Even in this dim light, Sunny could see the glint of tears in the man's eyes.

"So why are you selling him?" Sunny wanted to know. "Why don't you keep him?"

"Because I want him settled in a new life before I go to prison."

"Prison?" Sunny gasped. "Why are you going to prison?"

"For blowing up Bigg Manor," said Larry Smalls.

"You've blown up Bigg Manor!?!" said

Sunny. He was stunned.

"Not yet, I haven't," said Larry Smalls, his voice barely above a whisper. "But I'm about to."

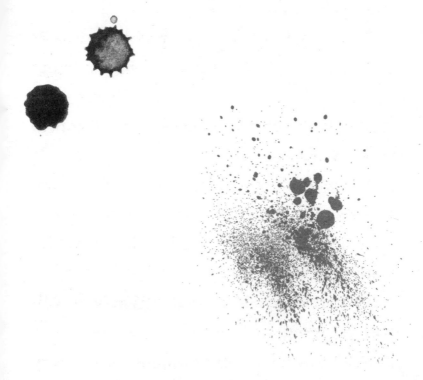

Chapter Twelve

Boom!
Boom!

Sunny found himself with more worries than he knew what to do with: Larry Smalls was planning to blow up Bigg Manor; he, Sunny, was about to take delivery of an elephant that they hadn't actually paid for; Larry Smalls was planning to blow up Bigg Manor; he might never see Mimi again; Larry Smalls was planning to blow up Bigg Manor; he didn't know what would become of Clip and Clop; and Larry Smalls was planning to blow up Bigg Manor.

Sunny's priorities were clear. He imagined sweet-smelling, bright-pink Mimi under a smouldering pile of bricks. "You can't go around blowing up houses, Mr Smalls!" he protested.

"Oh, but I can," said Larry Smalls. "The dynamite is in position and everything." His voice had gone back to sounding like the Larry Smalls Sunny had first met, preparing to throw those rocks at the gate of Bigg Manor.

"But Mimi . . . Mimi and the others!"

"I'm not planning on hurting anyone," said Larry Smalls. "I simply plan to reduce the house to rubble!"

"But what's the point?" protested Sunny.

"It's just an empty shell. Lord Bigg won't care and you'll go to prison for nothing."

"An empty shell?"

"Yes. Sack – he's the gardener – and Mimi – she's the boot boy – were telling me there's nothing in it. So all you'd be doing is destroying a useless building."

"It'll still be a Bold Statement though," said the ex-circus man. "It'll still Get People's Attention. Then I can tell the world what a crook Lord Bigg is!"

"But you can't blame today's Lord Bigg," said Sunny, trying to reason with him. "You said yourself that it was his *family* who started the business, hundreds of years ago, and, from what you say about his father and his father's father having to sell off stuff, they must have stopped making those useless railings long before he was b—"

A thought suddenly struck Sunny like a Scotch egg hits a frying pan (if you're playing tennis with them).

"What?" asked Larry Smalls. "What is it, Sunny?"

"The railings last ten years and a week before they go all floppy, right?"

"Right." Mr Smalls nodded. "Ten years and a week."

"But the last of the Bigg Railings must have been made long, long, ago. So surely the railings you used for your cage bars would have gone floppy and become useless long *before* you ever bought them! In fact, you wouldn't have bought them in the first place!"

"Which is EXACTLY why I hate this Lord Bigg so much," said Larry Smalls. "A while back, he actually managed to sell the factory but, before he did, he made *one last batch of railings* with the leftover metal lying around. And, even though he knew we were going to use them for cage bars, he sold them to the circus."

"But that's—"

"Criminal?"

"That's—"

"Outrageous?"

"That's WRONG!"

"Yes, Sunny. That's wrong," said Larry Smalls grimly. "He sold us railings for cage bars that he knew were unsafe, and animals – my animals – died because of it."

"But blowing up a building is wrong too," said Sunny.

"One thing at a time," said Smalls. "First, let's talk elephant." He pushed the barn door wide open and sunlight flooded the place, causing all three – two humans, one elephant

– to blink. He walked outside and Fingers followed, with Sunny close behind.

'But, Mr Smalls—"

"Elephant," he repeated.

Sunny gave a very sad sigh. "Mr Smalls, the truth is, I don't think my parents—"

"Those people really are your parents?" Larry Smalls interrupted.

"Sort of," said Sunny. "I don't know who my birth parents are."

"Aha." Smalls nodded.

"Anyway, I don't think they'd necessarily be the best people to look after Fingers. They're too . . ."

"Weird?" said Larry Smalls.

"Set in their ways," said Sunny. "They do everything *their* way."

"Then I want you to promise me something, Sunny."

"What?"

"Whether or not I blow up Bigg Manor – whether or not I go to prison – I want YOU to look after Fingers. He's yours now. So if you ever decide to part company with – with . . ."

Sunny supplied their names. "Mr and Mrs Grunt," he said.

"If ever you and the Grunts decide to go your separate ways, you must take Fingers with you. He's your responsibility. Is that a deal?"

Sunny was bubbling with excitement. His very own elephant! "But what if Dad has other ideas?"

"Don't worry about that," said Larry Smalls. He took Fingers' trunk in one hand and Sunny's hand in the other. Then he put them both together, Sunny curling his fingers round the end of the elephant's trunk. It was a bit like they were now holding hands, except that one of the hands was actually a trunk. "You two are together now, and Fingers knows it, don't you, boy?"

Fingers pulled the tip of his trunk from Sunny's grasp and put it round the boy's shoulders, giving him a kind of elephant hug. He knew it, all right.

"And even that Mr Grunt of yours isn't going to argue with an elephant, is he?"

Sunny supposed not. And now was the time to mention that the same Mr Grunt hadn't kept his part of the bargain.

"Mr Smalls—"

"No time," said Larry Smalls. "I've talked long enough and there's somewhere I have to be." The truth be told, he also hated long goodbyes. Now Fingers was safely in the care of the funny kid with the wonky ears and

blue dress, and the funny kid with the wonky ears and blue dress was safely in the care of Fingers, it was time for Larry Smalls to move on.

Of course, if Larry Smalls hadn't liked the look of whoever it was who was buying the elephant – he'd left those arrangements to Mr Lippy the clown – he would have kept Fingers, and simply wouldn't have kept *his* side of the bargain. This probably would have been a comfort to Sunny had he known it.

"But—"

"No, really, Sunny. This is goodbye." He jogged over to a pop-pop-pop motorcycle, over by a wire-mesh litter bin, and climbed on to the seat. "You'll find some bags of feed and caring instructions over there." He pointed. "Bye, Fingers!"

The elephant, standing by Sunny as if they

were old friends, his front leg pressed up against the boy's body, raised his trunk and waved.

"Come on, Fingers," said Sunny. "It's time to meet the Grunts."

Mr and Mrs Grunt couldn't have been more delighted when Sunny reappeared with the elephant. In fact, the boy couldn't remember a time when he'd seen them happier (and that included the day they managed to sink each and every remote-controlled boat at the annual Huntsworth Mayday Picnic).

"You've got him!" said Mr Grunt with such a smile.

"Hello, Fingers," said Mrs Grunt. She reached out and gave the elephant a hearty pat on the nearest part of him – a knee – which would have been enough to flatten an Irish wolfhound.

Fingers returned the compliment by feeling her hair with the tip of his trunk.

"That tickles!" said a delighted Mrs Grunt.

"Your head could do with a good hoovering!" said Mr Grunt. "Hope you don't give him fleas."

Sunny was forgotten in all the excitement so he slipped inside the caravan to look for his shoes. He found them in a box on the kitchen table labelled "JUNK", and put them back on his grass-stained feet.

When he went outside again, he found Mr Grunt leaning against Fingers as though he were a wall, chatting to the elephant. All the while, Fingers looked at him with his intelligent eyes.

"So no trouble with Mr Lippy then?" asked Mr Grunt when he saw the boy.

"No, Dad," said Sunny. "It was Mr Smalls who gave me Fingers, and I think everything's sort of OK, except for the fact that he plans to blow—"

"Who's Mr Smalls when he's at home?" demanded Mrs Grunt. "And what does he plan to blow? A raspberry? A kiss?"

"He's the man whose hat we threw rocks at," Sunny said. "The one who ended up hanging from the gates of Bigg Manor, and he's planning to blow—"

"Oh, him," said Mr Grunt with a raised eyebrow. "Small world."

"Small*s* world, more like," Mrs Grunt cackled. "I should be a comedian!"

"You're certainly a joke," said Mr Grunt.

"Dishcloth!" shouted Mrs Grunt.

"Earwax!" shouted Mr Grunt.

"Knuckle-head!" shouted Mrs Grunt.

"Herring!" shouted Mr Grunt.

That surprised Mrs Grunt. "You've never called me a herring before," she said quietly.

"I meant spongebag, you old spongebag!" said Mr Grunt.

Mrs Grunt seemed satisfied with that, and they carried on name-calling.

Sunny sighed and took Fingers over to a thistle patch to meet Clip and Clop. He knew he wouldn't get a word in edgeways when the Grunts were behaving like that, however urgent it was. The donkeys didn't seem at all bothered by a giant animal with a stretchy nose, and Fingers seem pleased to meet them. He sniffed their faces with his finger-like trunk. So, all in all, Sunny was happy with how that went.

It was then that he noticed a new trailer hitched to the back of the caravan. Not new as in shiny new, but new as in recently made, and new to Sunny. He'd never laid eyes on it before. It was very much in keeping with the caravan itself. It was made in the same style (or lack of style), as in loads-of-old-stuff-badly-put-together.

This must have been what all the hammering and bashing that was going on inside the caravan had been about. But what had Mr

Grunt built the trailer for? Storing elephant feed? Sunny seriously doubted that Mr Grunt would be that well organised.

"I see you're admiring my craftsmanship," said Mr Grunt, appearing at his side. He was wiping what appeared to be mud off one side of his face.

"Very nice," said Sunny. "What's it for?"

"What's it for? What's it *for*? Isn't it obvious what it's for?" asked Mr Grunt. He was trying to rub off the mud with an oily rag now.

"Not really, Dad," said Sunny, "which is why I asked."

"It's more of a *who* than a what," said Mrs Grunt. She had a mouthful of currant bun, having discovered the sack of them Larry Smalls had left for Sunny to feed Fingers.

"Who?" asked Sunny, wondering whether the "who" in question might actually be him, and that the trailer might be his very first bedroom. Sure, it was small and outdoors, but—

"It's for Clip and Clop, of course!" said Mrs Grunt. "Now that Fingers is going to pull our home, they can have a well-earned rest." She stared at Mr Grunt. "What's that all over your face, mister?"

"The remains of that mud you threw at me, wife!"

Mrs Grunt gave a triumphant leer, showing off her teeth – the yellow *and* the green ones – to great effect. "I had no idea I was such a good shot."

"Don't leer with your mouth full," grunted Mr Grunt, who'd seen more than enough half-chewed currant bun in hers.

Sunny, meanwhile, was feeling a flood of relief. So the two donkeys would still be part of the family. . .

Family.

Now, there was a word. Because, in their own strange way, of course, that's exactly what that odd collection of people and animals was: a family.

"A trailer for Clip and Clop! That's a great idea," said Sunny. Then he paused and took a deep breath. It was time to try again. "I know you're not big fans of helping people, but I really, really think we need to get to Bigg Manor as soon as possible—"

"Why on earth should we do that?" Mrs Grunt interrupted.

"The boy was about to tell us when you interrupted him," said Mr Grunt.

"Then shut up and let him speak," said Mrs Grunt.

"That's exactly what I was telling YOU to

do, wife!" fumed Mr Grunt.

"We need to warn them that someone is planning to blow up the house!" said Sunny.

"Blow it up?" said Mrs Grunt.

"YES!" said Sunny.

"Then of course we must go there," said Mrs Grunt.

"Definitely," said Mr Grunt. "I wouldn't want us to miss a good explosion. I love a good explosion!"

"Me too!" said Mrs Grunt, thinking back to her science lessons at school. "Come on!"

Now, Sunny could have wasted time arguing that the whole purpose of his getting to Bigg Manor as soon as possible was to try to STOP there being a big explosion, but a waste of time was all it would have been. With Mr and Mrs Grunt excited at the prospect of witnessing a big bang, Mrs Grunt was quick to get Clip and

Clop aboard their new custom-built trailer at the back, while Mr Grunt and Sunny hitched Fingers up to the newly adapted harness at the front of the caravan.

"A perfect fit!" said Mr Grunt. "Let's get going!"

So off they headed, a slightly puzzled Clip and Clop enjoying the view and feeling the wind whizzing between their ears, and an excited elephant pulling them at impressive speed, eager for adventure.

Chapter Thirteen
Law in Action

When they arrived at Bigg Manor, Sunny felt that they were as late as one could be without actually being too late. Sticking out of every window of the house was . . . was . . .

"Dynamite!" Sunny gasped.

Up above the rooftop, brilliantly coloured birds circled and swooped, and squawked in dismay. Sunny could clearly make out Monty, the parrot that had been eyeing his nose in the potting shed, his beautiful plumage catching the fading rays of the sun.

There was no difficulty in Fingers pulling the Grunts' caravan, trailer and all, up the drive because the gates – those hated gates – hung crooked, broken and wide open where something had rammed them apart. One of the lion-topped pillars was badly scraped, the fresh scars showing white against the weathered stone, where something had hit it hard. And that something was stationed on the lawn before them now, right by the pond where Mimi had hidden from the bees.

It was a giant of a mechanical digger with a huge yellow scoop on the front with jagged teeth of metal. And it was in that scoop – now raised in its highest position – that Larry Smalls stood. Yes, he was wearing his BIGG AIN'T BEST T-shirt but (quite apart from the crazy glint in his eyes) there was something very different about him: it was the bow and

arrow he was brandishing. Instead of being pointy, the tip of the arrow was wrapped in cloth. And, from the way that the cloth was burning, it had obviously been dipped in something . . . something like *petrol*.

Sunny could see the servants crowding round the base of the digger. There was Sack the gardener, Jack the handyman (also known as Handyman Jack) and a woman he took to be Jack's wife, Agnes the cook and maid, and someone else – a spiky red-haired man – who must be Peach the butler.

There was no sign of Mimi. Sunny gulped. Was she still inside the building?

He had already jumped down from the caravan and was rushing towards the digger. The servants were being prevented from reaching Larry Smalls by a small but dedicated group of ex-circus performers.

Jeremy the juggler was running up and down, juggling flaming clubs and nasty-looking knives. There was also a very large man who had no neck to speak of – his head just seemed to join his body – who was wearing

a beautifully tailored pink-striped shirt, and a frightening expression on his face. He was bending enormous metal bars as if they were as floppy as Lord Bigg's ten-year-and-one-week-old railings. And there was Mr Lippy, in full clown clobber – including a squirty plastic rose on his lapel – cycling around the digger on a tiny bicycle, firing green gunk from a super-soaker at anyone foolish enough to try to get too near.

Hitched to the front of the Grunts' caravan, Fingers caught sight of his old friend Mr Smalls, raised his trunk and let out a mournful trumpet.

Larry Smalls turned and saw Sunny and the others. "Oh, you came!" he shouted. "And you're just in time!"

"Wait!" shouted Sunny. "Where are Mimi and Lord Bigg? How can you be sure the house is empty?! WAIT!"

"Fire the arrow! Fire the arrow!" shouted Mr and Mrs Grunt in an unusual example of unity. "Do it now! Do it now! Do it now!" they chanted.

There was sudden movement at the right-hand side of the house, and Sunny could make out two figures climbing from a window on the middle floor and shimmying down a drainpipe with the speed and agility of acrobats.

The Chinn Twins! thought Sunny. *It must be the Chinn Twins!*

And how right he was. Having reached the lawn, the Chinns were now cartwheeling and somersaulting to a safe distance.

"Ready?" shouted Larry Smalls from on high.

"Ready!" replied the far-off voices of the twins.

"This is for the animals of Smalls' Big Top!" cried Larry Smalls. But Sunny hadn't been idle all this time. As far as he knew, water put out flames, and what was that fish pond over there filled with? Plenty of the wet stuff. He knew from an article (in a newspaper that Mr Grunt had used to wrap up a dead badger before cooking) that elephants were good at sucking up water in their trunks and spraying it everywhere. So all he needed to do was to combine the two: to get Fingers to suck up the water from the fish pond and to squirt out Mr Smalls' blazing arrow . . .

. . . but Sunny wasn't altogether sure where Fingers' loyalty lay. Certainly, he and Fingers were together now, but the elephant had years of history with Larry Smalls and, even if Fingers *was* now loyal to him rather than Larry, he didn't feel too comfortable about making him act against his old friend Larry's wishes.

What decided it for Sunny was Mimi. Or the absence of Mimi. For all Sunny knew, she was inside the manor stuffed to the gills with dynamite, about to be blown to smithereens.

So Sunny hurried Fingers to the fish pond and the elephant sucked up water at incredible speed. Sunny turned Fingers to face Larry Smalls . . . but it was too late.

As the jet of water squirted from the perfectly aimed elephant trunk towards the flaming arrow tip, Larry Smalls let loose the arrow and it arched through the air landing gracefully

in the wide-open front doorway, where it spluttered and sparked, before erupting into the first of a sequence of stupendous explosions.

"NO!" screamed Sunny.

"Nice one!" screamed Mrs Grunt.

"Yay!" shouted Mr Grunt.

Handyman Jack, Peaches, Agnes and Sack stopped trying to reach Larry Smalls now – there was little point; the damage was done – and they turned to watch the spectacle. Mr Lippy stopped pedalling the tiny tricycle, Jeremy stopped his dangerous juggling, and Trunk ceased the bar-bending and grimacing (though he continued to wear his very nice pink-striped shirt). All eyes were on the big event.

As they watched open-mouthed, Lord Bigg

suddenly appeared at a window and – without so much as a second glance down – jumped. If Lady "La-La" Bigg hadn't at that self-same moment appeared round the side of the manor – presumably from the pigsty – with Poppet the pig in hot pursuit, he may well have done himself a serious injury. As it was, he landed directly on top of the pig, who seemed more disgruntled – and grunty – than damaged by the whole experience.

But there was something odd about these explosions. All but one of the onlookers were expecting crumbling masonry and thick black smoke as Bigg Manor collapsed in an inferno. But instead, as each stick of so-called dynamite ignited, it shot in the air – or wherever it could – with a trailing of glittering sparks, like a firework . . . which was hardly surprising because that's exactly what they were: fireworks.

As everyone suddenly realised that they were watching a fabulous firework display, the mood of the onlookers changed. The servants, Jeremy and Mr Lippy started "Oooo"-ing and "Ahhhh"-ing. Trunk looked absolutely delighted, and a childish grin spread across his face. Sunny let out a sigh of relief, and even Mr and Mrs Grunt settled down on the grass to watch. But Larry Smalls was incandescent with rage. If you didn't know what "incandescent" meant, you do now, because that was just how blood-vessel-burstingly, humongously ANGRY Larry Smalls was.

Standing in the scoop of the metal-toothed digger, he grabbed fistfuls of his BIGG AIN'T BEST T-shirt and began tearing it apart with his bare hands. Soon it was little more than tattered shreds, revealing his string vest beneath. He howled. He ranted. He screamed. He yelled. Then he sat down with a thud and started to sob. It was at this point that three police cars arrived, sirens blaring and lights

flashing (which is exactly what you want from a police car, really). Sitting in the front passenger seat of the first car was none other than Mimi, with Frizzle and Twist humming round her head as usual.

Sunny dashed forward as she clambered out of her seat. "You're all right!" he yelped. Although he'd been worried about everyone at the manor, he'd been worried about the sweet-smelling, extraordinarily pink Mimi most of all.

"All right? Yes, I'm all right," she said distractedly, looking up at the whiz-bangs in the sky. "Fireworks!" She gawped. "They're nothing but fireworks! I told the police it was dynamite!" For it was Mimi who had grabbed Handyman Jack's tricycle and pedalled as fast as she could to the local police station. While the others had been running round in a what-

shall-we-do kind of way,
she'd taken pink, sweet-smelling action.

And a tricycle.

"We *all* thought it was dynamite!" said Sunny and before she knew what was happening, he gave her a big hug. Before he knew what was happening, she gave him one right back. The hummingbirds hovered above them both.

The police, meanwhile, had poured out of all three cars and were charging about trying to look busy and important, and enjoying the free show.

"Who's in charge here?" shouted a policeman, a bent-nosed, cauliflower-eared man by the name of Brown.

"I am!" boomed Lord Bigg, wearing his dressing gown, which had a perfect impression of a pig – legs splayed out sideways – on the front, in mud. "I demand that you make arrests immediately!" His sticking-plastered face looked even stranger in the blue glow of the police cars' flashing lights.

"This is your property, sir?" said Inspector Brown, eyes narrowing. He was staring at the dressing gown with great interest.

"Yes, yes. I am Lord Bigg. This is Bigg Manor."

"And do you have a licence for this firework display, sir?"

"I am not a 'sir', I am a 'lord'! And no, of course I don't have a licence for this . . . this . . . *display*, you nincompoop!" Lord Bigg spluttered.

It's never a good idea to call a policeman a nincompoop. "Turn round, please, Your

Lordship," said Inspector Brown, scratching his bent nose.

"WHAT?" demanded Lord Bigg.

"You heard me, Your Lordship. Turn round, please," said the policeman.

"I will not!" said Lord Bigg.

"That wasn't a request," said Inspector Brown. "I am instructing you to turn round in the name of the law!"

"This is preposterous," said Lord Bigg, but something in the policeman's voice suggested that he might punch Bigg on the nose if he didn't do as he was told. So he turned round.

When the policeman saw the words BARNEY "THE BRUISER" BROWN

written in nice big letters on the back of Lord Bigg's dressing gown, he nodded in an I-thought-so kind of way . . . because he thought he'd recognised that dressing gown the minute he clapped eyes on it, Poppet-the-pig-shaped mud stain or no Poppet-the-pig-shaped mud stain.

"Lord Bigg, I am arresting you for holding an illegal firework display and on suspicion of theft or of receiving stolen goods—" began Brown.

"STOLEN GOODS?" Lord Bigg bellowed. "What stolen goods?"

"Is your name by any chance Barney 'The Bruiser' Brown, My Lord?"

"Of course it isn't, you . . . you buffoon!"

"I thought not, Lord Bigg. Because *I* am Barney 'The Bruiser' Brown and that's MY dressing gown you're wearing."

"Oh," said Lord Bigg, his mouth itself forming the shape of a little "o". There wasn't much he could say to that.

"And not only am I the rightful owner of that dressing gown," Inspector Brown added, "I am also arresting you." He sounded rather happy about it.

Moments later, Lord Bigg found himself being led away in handcuffs.

Larry Smalls witnessed the whole thing from his excellent vantage point up in the digger scoop, his eyes filling with tears of joy. Soon he was whooping with delight, which led to Jeremy the juggler, Trunk the strongman, Mr

Lippy the clown, and the Remarkable Chinn Twins to whoop too, and before they could stop themselves the Bigg Manor servants – including Mimi – found themselves whooping, which started Sunny off, which finally made Fingers start trumpeting, and everyone burst into song.

"Do you have a licence to hold an outdoor concert on your premises?" Inspector Brown asked Lord Bigg in the back of the police car.

"Of course I don't have a— Er, no, officer," said Lord Bigg, ending more meekly than he'd begun.

"Then I'm afraid I'm going to have to add it to my list of charges," said Inspector Brown, looking very pleased indeed.

Chapter Fourteen

All Change

Once the police cars had gone, Sunny turned to Mr Grunt. "Dad?" he said. "You know that stuff you gave to Larry Smalls in return for Fingers, which wasn't quite what you'd promised it would be?"

"Yes," said Mr Grunt with a grunt.

"You didn't promise him dynamite and give him fireworks instead, by any chance, did you?"

"Might have," said Mr Grunt. And he might even have smiled. Larry Smalls had climbed down from the digger, and now strode across to them both. He'd removed the remains of his BIGG AIN'T BEST T-shirt and was now wearing a colourful one emblazoned with the words "SMALLS' BIG TOP" across the front. He gripped Mr Grunt's hand and shook it.

"I couldn't be happier with today's outcome," he said. "I couldn't be happier!"

Mr Grunt put his free hand on Larry Smalls' arm. "I'm pleased for you," he said. "Does that mean you don't want the elephant back?"

"He's Sunny's now," said Mr Smalls.

"Sunny's?" said Mr Grunt.

Larry Smalls nodded. "And Bigg is in trouble! Bigg is in *BIG* trouble! I couldn't be happier . . ." The delighted ex-circus owner turned and strode off, humming a victory march.

Just then, a large woman with a large,

wide-brimmed, flowery-crowned hat came bounding over, closely followed by an even fatter (and extremely muddy) pig. They both stared up at Fingers with interest.

"Hello!" she snorted. "So they carted off the old man, did they?"

"If you mean Lord Bigg, then yes," said Sunny.

"Excellent! Excellent!" she snorted. "Glad to see the back of the pompous old plaster-face. All he cared about were his silly old birds."

Sunny didn't know what to say, so said nothing.

"I'm Lady Bigg," said the woman, "but you can call me La-La! This little poppet is Poppet." She pointed down at the far-from-little pig, who was still looking up at Fingers in amazement. She'd never *seen* such a big pig (or what she *thought* was a pig).

"Oink," said Poppet.

"Trumpet," said Fingers.

"Oink," said Poppet. She was in love.

La-La Lady Bigg looked around. "Peach!"

she called. "PEACH!"

The red-haired butler appeared out of the chaos. "You yelled, m'lady?" he said.

"You're fired," she said.

Sunny was SHOCKED. She'd seemed such a nice lady and now she was kicking the butler out of his job.

"You, Agnes, Handyman Jack, Sack and Mimi. The lot of you. You can leave any time you wish," she went on.

"We can?" said Peach, raising a bushy red eyebrow in surprise.

"If you likc. You're welcome to stay if you *want* to, any of you, but otherwise you can just go!"

Sunny smiled. Now she was making sense.

"But our contracts, m'lady," said Peach. "His Lordship made it absolutely clear that if we left we'd be in breach of contract, and that he could sue us for every penny—"

At that moment, the flames must have found a new batch of fireworks. There was a series of bang-bang-bangs and the skies filled with a whole new shower of multicoloured sparks.

"Sue you for every penny you *don't have* in the first place?" asked La-La.

Peach smiled. "You have a point there, m'lady."

"And do you know where the contracts are, Peach?"

The butler nodded.

"Then tear 'em up, Peach! I'm moving out of the pigsty and back into the manor! With the boring old plaster-face out of the way, things are going to change around here." Lady Bigg turned back to Sunny. "And who are you?" she asked. "You do look rather familiar . . . and I like your elephant."

"Thank you," said Sunny. "And I like your pig."

"You're not my son, are you? Only I lost him a long time back and he must be your age by now."

"No," said Mrs Grunt, barging between them. "This is my boy, Sunny."

"Yes," said Mr Grunt. "This is Sunny, our son."

"Just wondered," said Lady Bigg with a shrug. "It's nothing to get het up about, is it, Poppet?" She patted her beloved pig.

Sunny was about to protest – what if he *was* Horace? – when La-La went on: "Whoever you are, you and your elephant and family and friends are all welcome to stay at Bigg Manor as long as you like. You all are."

There were claps and cheers and more whoops of delight, some from the servants, who Peach had just told about the tearing up of the contracts.

Mimi turned to Sunny. "You know," she said. "I might like it here if I don't have to be the boot boy. I think I might stay."

And stay they all did, even the Grunts. But matters didn't end there. Of course they didn't. Lord Bigg wasn't under lock and key for ever, though he did end up in jail for a long time. Then there was the fact that wherever the Grunts went, trouble was never far behind and when they *didn't* go anywhere, trouble soon found them anyway.

Like the first time they ran out of elephant-feed and decided to take the caravan to Hunnybun's Bun Factory to stock up on – you guessed it – some currant buns (stale ones if they were cheaper). It took them past a very pretty thatched cottage with a messed-up front garden. Although Mr Grunt wasn't sure he recognised it, he found his bottom tingling at the memory of being peppered with peppercorns . . .

. . . and before he could say, "Silly old bat!",

Elsie Spawn had her blunderbuss pointing out of the window, ready to fire.

What she hadn't bargained for was a smart elephant, such as Fingers. Before she'd even had the satisfaction of pulling the trigger, a large trunk had wrapped itself around the weapon's trumpet-like muzzle and had pulled it from her grasp.

"Monster!" she bellowed, peering over the windowsill. "Brute! Ogre!" Because, in all the good ways, Sunny was nothing like Mr and Mrs Grunt, he made sure that Fingers returned the weapon to the elderly lady – once he'd tipped out the gunpowder and drawing pins – but, the truth be told, it never worked again. Fingers' elephantine grip had left the muzzle all crudnuckled (which isn't a real word, but one that best describes the state it was in).

The delay meant that they didn't reach the

Hunnybun's factory until after closing time.

"It's all your fault!" Mrs Grunt shouted from the bedroom window.

"Yours!" Mr Grunt shouted back from the factory's sloping forecourt. He wanted to kick something, and chose a piece of wood. It was a large cheese-shaped wedge under the back wheel of a delivery van. He kicked it clear. The van began rolling slowly backwards towards him.

"Look out, mister!" Mrs Grunt shouted from the caravan, before she could stop herself.

"What?" shouted Mr Grunt. "How do you expect me to hear you when you MUMBLE, wife?"

"Nothing!" Mrs Grunt replied, with a flash of green and yellow teeth.

Mr Grunt grunted, and only jumped clear thanks to Sunny's last-minute warning cry of,

"Dad!"

The van rumbled past him and hit a bollard, causing its back doors to burst open. Sunny read the words on the nearest one: SUPPLIERS OF FRESH HONEY TO HUNNYBUN'S.

What Mr Grunt said next was drowned out by a sudden loud buzzing noise, but Sunny could guess what it was. It was a single word, shouted loud and long. It was: *"Beeeeeeeeee eeeeeeeeeeeeeeeeeeeeeeeeees!"*